Portland

Short Stories

Raud Kennedy

Also by Raud Kennedy

Gnawing the Bone: Dog Fiction
Mad Rabbits
Stick Out Your Tongue
Top of the World
Streaking Venus
Sex on the Beach
Twice Dead
Black Oak
Glimpses – Poems

Portland

Short Stories

Raud Kennedy

Cover photos by Manson Kennedy
ISBN-13: 978-1463521738
ISBN-10: 1463521731
www.raudkennedy.com

Portland

Short Stories

Contents

Portland

A man in a printed flower dress,
a winter coat with a faux fur hood,
pushes a Safeway shopping cart
through the rain down Broadway.
Another man, sideburns to his jaw,
a navy suit jacket over dungarees,
reads the ads for teeth whitener
in a Fred Meyer's newspaper insert
like they were stock quotes.
He moves around the intersection,
a minute hand going corner to corner,
acting out this same tableau.
A bearded lady in running shoes
passes with her dachshunds.
Lyndon Johnson, black as a mortician.
A homeless man as a gnome.
No, it is a gnome. Homeless.

Silver Elvis

"I like raw sugar sprinkled on my nipples," Heather said, smiling, her lips glistening with maple syrup from her pancakes. Her voice matched her name, subtle flowers covering a hillside. Her last name was Honeysuckle and her perfume scented the air around her like the flowers in spring. She took another bite of pancakes and chewed. People at work, including Jonathon, who sat across from her in Weber's Diner, wondered why she wasn't morbidly obese. She ate whatever she wanted whenever she wanted it; chocolate maple bars, fresh baked cinnamon rolls, banana splits overflowing with whipped cream. Instead she was a tall waif who eschewed flaunting her looks.

Heather had a nighttime obsession. Once the sun dropped behind the coast range, she'd disappear into the darkness and run for miles, only to be seen by the occasional flash of passing headlights: thin legs, reflective shoes, skinny top showing off her pierced bellybutton. She wore a crystal in it the size of a marble that sparkled when the light hit it right.

Heather really liked Jonathon. He laughed at her jokes and made her laugh in kind, and he was cute in a pudgy sort of way. Everyone at the bakery where they both worked was pudgy. It came with the job, a nibble here, a nibble there. What's another croissant with your coffee in the morning or during your afternoon break? Another pastry, or a donut, and your belly button sank deeper and deeper until it swallowed up whatever you had it pierced with. But not Heather, though Jonathon was pushing past pudgy. She was trying to think of a nice way to put it. She wanted one of those phrases that said fat but meant important, like his weight gave him gravitas, but Jonathon didn't have gravitas. She would've thought he was gay if she didn't know he wasn't. He was the jolly fat man who loved to tease.

"What about your nipples? Are they sensitive, too?" she asked.

He was thinking about Heather's nipples and how sensitive they might be. He didn't care about his own. As far as he was concerned he didn't have any. "Oh yes, very sensitive, the slightest breeze and they—" but he wasn't talking about his own.

"Shut up! I can't help it." Her nipples always drew glances and comments in the bakery. The ovens kept the room warm, so when she'd step outside to cool off, she'd return with grapes in her shirt. "My mother used to make me wear Band Aids. Until even she gave up and stopped noticing. Well, are they?"

"Sensitive?" He sipped his coffee. "I don't have nipples. I was abducted by aliens as a child and they stole them. I wonder what they needed them for. Maybe they collect them."

"Collect them?"

"If I were you, I'd be running scared. You're sporting the jewels of their collection."

"People don't sport nipples."

"Ah yes, but not everyone is you. Believe me, you sport them."

Their conversation paused as they ate, and then Heather asked, "Have you had any more of those weird dreams recently?" She tore open a packet of sugar, poured it over her moistened finger into her coffee and stuck her finger in her mouth with a wink at him. "Well?"

"Not since the silver Elvis." He'd had a string of vivid dreams lately, all of them entailing small, two-legged creatures running about his bedroom. He'd wake up and in that state between being asleep and not yet fully awake, the little devils would scatter and try to hide, but then as he became fully awake they would fade into the dim light and were no longer there. He didn't know what to make of these experiences so he used them to entertain his friends. Silver Elvis was a small guy wearing a shiny silver suit, like Elvis used to wear for his Las Vegas shows, that Jonathon had woken up to sitting on his bed. When Silver Elvis saw that he'd been spotted he jumped off the bed and hid at the foot of it. He wasn't very good at hiding, but he was saved by Jonathon coming fully awake.

Another time he woke to see a small monkey in a Day-Glo pink spacesuit crawling across his ceiling. When it saw him move in his bed below, it zipped down the hall ceiling like a crab on speed and disappeared into the bathroom, never to be seen again. It wore gold goggles that went well with the suit. These dreams were strange, but they didn't trouble him, even if they were a little too real. He'd had others that were disturbing that he didn't use as fodder for his funny stories, true X-Files material that he pushed out of his mind as a result of too much pizza before going to bed.

Heather stirred her coffee, took a sip, and then added more cream. If she was going to drink it, it had to be just right. She sensed Jonathon wanted something from her. He'd been more attentive recently, a little too focused on her. She hoped he hadn't gotten a crush on her. She didn't want to lose him as a friend because he thought he was falling in love with her when it was really just because he was horny and she was the kind of woman who gave men wood. She stared at him without saying anything.

"What?" he asked.

Not one to leave it be, she said, "Do you have a crush on me?"

He was hesitant. "If I do, is that bad?"

"I knew it. Damn it."

"Heather, I've had a crush on you since I first saw you. I'm a guy and you're gorgeous. Every guy at work has a crush on you and at one point or another has said how much they'd love to slip it to you. Something would be wrong with me if I didn't have a crush on you." He stopped and smiled at her. "Why? Do you have a crush on me? Because that would complicate things. I don't like to shit where I eat. You've probably confused love for lust." He put his palms on his belly and gave it a lift. "If I'd known you were a chubby chaser."

"Slip it to me?"

* * *

The night passed under her feet like a fast-flowing creek in spring. She moved through the fog, an apparition of the night, her footfalls landing almost without sound. The loop at the top of the hill was a different world. She went around it in a meditative state, a feather in the wind. She ran by the houses with their people buttoned up inside, tucked into their beds under their electric blankets, sleeping or dreaming or struggling to do one but not the other. Heather dreamed, but she dreamed when she was awake and rarely when she was asleep. She once dreamed of being a country music singer in the 1950s. In the dream she was in her car listening to herself sing on the radio. She was singing about a guy she exchanged glances with at a bus station whom she thought was the one but who got on a different bus so she never found out if he had been.

Heather didn't listen to music when she ran. She followed the sound of her feet, her breaths, the wind through her thoughts. She didn't want lyrics to direct where they went. Her thoughts were her own and she rarely felt like piggy-backing on someone else's. People's minds were filled with other people's thoughts enough as it was; what was popular, what wasn't, or who. There were miniskirt fads, black nail polish fixations, mullets, metrosexuals. She wondered how much of people's thoughts were their own and not absorbed opinions of others. Top one hundred lists like "America's Most Powerful Opinion Makers," made her wince. That was her gripe with television. Its main purpose seemed to be to shape people's opinions, and in some cases not only to shape them but to create the thoughts that led to the opinions. When she quit watching television she lost a lot of common ground with people. She no longer kept up with the imaginary people's lives and couldn't discuss them while kneading bread dough with the others. When she listened to the others talk about them she had to remind herself that they were talking about people who weren't real. If people were talking about something that never happened, did their conversation ever happen? She'd tease herself with thoughts like that, which only made her more estranged from the conversation. When she brought up real things in conversation it only proved to be uncomfortable, so she learned to keep her thoughts to herself and talk about sugar on her nipples instead.

* * *

It was true. Jonathon had fallen in love with her and he knew it was bad for their friendship. It was becoming difficult to be around her, and it wasn't just lust, though he did lust after her. The jolly fat man and the hot chick wasn't going to happen.

People said looks weren't important but everyone knew that was bullshit. He'd have to be rich and she'd have to sell her soul for his riches. The state of his body revealed a lot about how he felt about his life, about himself and where he wanted to go.

He was at an impasse. He knew he could take out his frustration and his unrequited love in his usual way by eating another donut and packing on a few more pounds—he'd gained thirty-five since meeting her—but he couldn't con himself with that any longer. That feeling of being satiated on calories wasn't cutting it anymore. It was time to make a break and he felt it inside, so he put the donut back in the box with the rest of the dozen and closed the lid. He was going to have to find an activity other than eating to take the edge off his frustration and loneliness.

* * *

She ran through the night fog, eddies swirling in the light under the street lamps behind her. She was rapidly overtaking another runner ahead of her, a big man trudging along at a methodical, determined pace. She smiled at the sight of someone else nutty enough to run at night in terrible conditions. As she passed the man a sideway glimpse reminded her of Jonathon, but that couldn't be, and she was soon far ahead and her thoughts were elsewhere.

I'll Show You Where to Put It

Fatso felt a tightness in his head. It didn't hurt like a headache or the onset of a migraine. It felt like his brain was encased in a condom, and someone was tying a knot at the end, sealing him in like a goldfish in a Glad sandwich bag on its way out the pet shop door. He woke shackled spread eagle to the bolster and footboard of his bed. Then it all came back to him. He'd been overwhelmed with boredom on his way home, so he stopped in at the Spot, a tavern with mold in the bathrooms, where he could have a beer and not be bothered. But that hadn't been enough. The boredom clung to him like the mold on the tiles and he tried to shake it off with a few more beers, and when that seemed to be working, he no longer felt like going home, and went clubbing instead. He remembered dancing at Dante's, a nightclub with an entryway that reeked of bum urine, and drinking tequila poppers and Jägermeister, and then the girl. He even remembered her name, Blondie.

At least he was shackled in his own bedroom with his own handcuffs. They were a black pair he'd bought recently at Spartacus's Leather and Toys, and he was pretty sure the spare key was still in the nightstand only inches away. Then the adrenal surge flushed over him as he saw that his wallet was missing from its usual place on his nightstand, and he realized he'd been robbed, again. Boredom always got him into trouble.

It was one of the Portland Tower maids who found him prostrate on his bed. His morning erection had gone limp long ago, but he was still embarrassed. Fatso was lucky she was scheduled to clean his unit, or else he could've been stuck there for days calling out to be set free as he wilted from thirst and exposure. If his neighbors had heard him, they would've ignored him. He called out a lot when he had guests over; they were that sort of guests, guests who left the elevator smelling of perfume, sweat and cigarettes. His neighbors had considered complaining to the management about him, but complaining about your neighbor's sexual peccadilloes infringing on your living environment would be frowned upon. Besides, the Portland Towers were an adult living facility. That was made clear in the rental agreement where condoms were encouraged and children were discouraged.

Fatso made it to work on time, thanks to the maid. Not that it would've mattered if he'd been late. He owned the health club where he worked, Fatso's. Fatso wasn't so fat anymore, but the name had stuck, and so had a few of his old insecurities. He had the body of an underwear model, but during his walks to work he often thought his reflection in the storefront windows was someone else. He'd look over his shoulder to see who was there, but he'd be all alone. Though in a way there was someone else there. He still saw himself as a supersized fast food drive thru type of guy, not the obsessive, calorie counting, work out every day sort of guy. He still had his fat man clothes, afraid that he might yet still need them. When he felt really blue, he'd put them on and laugh at how big they were. It would cheer him up and he'd get on with dealing with whatever was making him blue.

That afternoon he went straight home after leaving the gym, put on his sixty-inch-waist pants and sat on his bed trying to cheer himself up. But it wasn't working. He was hungover, though no more than in the past, when it had worked. He vowed not to go on another bender, but he knew that would only last until the boredom got to him again, and he'd have to go stir up drama in his life by being a fuckup. Why fight it, he wondered. Why not embrace the stupid things he did since he obviously did them for a reason.

Then it came to him why he was still blue even after putting on his fat man pants. It was the girl, Blondie. Normally his pick ups were just physical attractions that led to a little role playing to prolong the inevitable wham, bam, thank you ma'am. But he liked her and was hurt that she didn't like him back enough not to steal from him. Portland wasn't a big city, and its nightlife was even smaller. On a thin party circuit like this one, if she went out at all, he was bound to run into her again. What went around, came around, and he'd be there to watch her step in it. Now that he was feeling spiteful he felt better. He liked this plan. It implied that there was justice in his world, but also, though he wouldn't admit it even to himself, he liked it because he could now rationalize going out clubbing anytime he liked with the excuse of looking for his retribution. Even tonight. It would make him feel better, looking for her, working to get even. There was also that craving for the hair of the dog, but first he'd go to the gym again as an extra precaution against guilt and self-recrimination.

* * *

She'd have to watch it when it came to the Portland Towers, Blondie thought. Fatso wasn't the first guy she'd ripped off who lived there. They must've rented exclusively to dumb drunks who took their loaded willies out for a spin once a week. Well, he deserved to pay. It wasn't that the sex with him hadn't been enjoyable, or that he'd been objectionable. When she got up to leave, his wallet was on the nightstand there for the taking. On impulse she simply put it into her bag with her fishnet stockings and her other things she was gathering up off the floor by the bed. It had been second nature, like picking up a penny on the sidewalk. Ninety-nine more and she'd have a dollar. He deserved it for leaving it out where she could see it. That was stupid. He was stupid; nice, but stupid. A smart person hid their money at night. She did. She hid it where no one could find it without waking her.

Which is what she did now as she climbed into her bed to sleep the afternoon away before she went in to dance on the pole at the Stumptown Cabaret. She earned serious money there. Sure, she had to rub her buns in the customers' laps, feel their stiffies in her crack, and listen to their titty bar jokes she'd heard a thousand times before, but it was the art of the tease and she took pride in—stringing them along from song to song, keeping them hard until she'd cleaned them out and they had to leave. She avoided the Champagne route where the customer paid a boatload of money for a bottle of cheap sparkling wine and she was expected to sit there and share it. The club pitched this as a way to spend "quality time" with your favorite dancer, but it was far from a quality time for her. Talking to the customer would be like conversing with the cow before you slaughtered it. Besides, the house took 60 percent of the take on the bottle of wine while Blondie did all the work.

That evening when she entered the club's dressing room, the first thing she heard was a chunky dancer who went by the stage name of Trixie say, "If he loves me, he'll marry me and take me away from all this to the good life. I know he can afford to. He drives a really big BMW and always wears a hundred percent silk tie."

Trixie's girlfriend, whose stage name was Sindy, smacked her Bubblicious gum a few times, thinking there had to be a flaw in her friend's plan. "And if he won't marry you?"

Trixie checked her pigtails in the mirror that ran the length of the dressing room. She and Sindy were a dance duo who worked the Catholic school uniform fetish. They danced as little as possible and preferred the Champagne bucket, which in their case often served a dual purpose by the end of the night. Trixie applied some more lip gloss, puckered her lips in an empty kiss and answered, "Then I'll get an abortion. It won't be the first one, and in the meantime"—she cupped her breasts in her hands—"I'll get better tips because my tits are full of milk."

Sindy scrunched up her face in mock pain. "But don't abortions hurt?"

"Not if you don't think about it."

Trixie and Sindy were loud like the schoolgirls they portrayed. All the dancers in the room were forced to listen to their nonstop inanities. Blondie was having a tough time tuning them out as she tightened her black corset. She closed her eyes and tried to calm herself with thoughts of pigeons. They're only pigeons, she said to herself, nothing to give a second thought to.

Sindy smacked her gum some more, thinking. The air around her smelled like Passion Fruit flavor. "Maybe he loves us both because I gave him a handjob under the table last week."

Trixie stopped blowing herself kisses in the mirror and turned on her stool to look at her friend. "You did?"

Sindy nodded and chewed her Bubblicious. She didn't see the slap coming.

"You stupid cow!" Trixie shouted.

Cindy fell backward off her stool and lay there rubbing her cheek. "There was nothing wrong with it. He paid me for it," she said sullenly.

Blondie couldn't take it anymore. The pigeons were shitting everywhere. Kill the pigeons. They were making her more depressed than she already was. "Hey, bobbysocks, enough already. None of us want to hear your drama."

"No kidding," a few of the other dancers said in agreement.

Trixie, the pregnant one, stood up and puffed out her chest. "Well if it isn't the high and mighty Blondie. Mind your own business, bitch, or I'll string you up with that pretty long hair of yours."

Blondie knew speaking to her wouldn't do any good, but she didn't want to speak to her anyway. She wanted her to crawl off to a corner and be quiet. Their dumpy schoolgirl shtick was nothing compared to her own shtick as a corseted dominatrix. From her bag she took a black bullwhip that was more than a prop. She'd stolen it from the nightstand of a lion tamer retired from the circus and she prided herself on her skill with it. She let it loose to the floor, then cracked it over Trixie's head. "Not another word," she said quietly.

Trixie puffed out her chubby chest even more. "You wouldn't dare."

Still rubbing her cheek, Sindy slowly shook her head and said, "Big mistake."

In that moment, Blondie snapped. If she'd been in the Oval Office with her finger on the bomb, she would've blown up the world. "I so would dare," she said as she brought the whip high over her head and cracked it across Trixie's chest, leaving a bright red mark on her pasty skin.

Trixie yelped and jiggled out of the dressing room and was quickly followed by Sindy. Now that it was quiet, the other dancers went back to putting on their faces, but Blondie knew this false sense of normalcy wouldn't last. Later, when she was out on the club floor grinding her ass in the lap of an old man, hardly feeling a bump, the club manager stepped in front of her. His name was Humberto, but all the girls in the club called him Suckit behind his back because he'd pretty much asked all of them at one time or another to suck his dick. Many had when they got in a jam at the club, but not Blondie. She despised him and all who would fellate him.

"I knew you'd fuck up with that whip," he said. "Get your gear and clear out. You're through here."

She kept grinding as she looked up at Suckit hoping to get some sort of rise out of her customer, but maybe her heart wasn't in it, or her ass. "Don't you want to hear my side of it?"

"I've warned you before about fighting with the other girls. You're a bad influence."

She felt a response in the old man's lap that brought a smile to her lips. "That schoolgirl bitch ran to your office and sucked you off, didn't she?"

He looked away and wouldn't meet her gaze. "Just get your stuff and get going," he said and faded into the darkness of the club's shadows.

It wasn't the first time she'd been fired and as long as she had to deal with people like Trixie and Suckit, it wouldn't be the last. The song ended and she collected from the old man who was now showing a definite lump in his double knit slacks.

"Are you sure you can't stay and dance for me again?" he asked in his nicest grandpa voice. Put a beard on him and he could be Santa.

She smiled. "Sorry. Think of me when you get home, pops."

Chubby Trixie had won, but next time when she wanted to get her way it would cost her more than a hummer. She'd be bent over Suckit's desk on a daily basis until he got bored of her dimpled cheeks. Trixie could say goodbye to being swept away from this life to a new one of plenty by the guy in the silk tie and BMW. It was more likely she'd be swept out the door with the cigarette butts and refuse, all danced out with no place to go. But not to worry. A pimp would find her and infuse her life with new purpose. Pimps had a sixth sense for finding girls like her. They could smell the desperation from miles away.

Blondie got her stuff out of the dressing room and left. She didn't need the job anyway. She'd saved enough money to last her a year without working if she wished. But she didn't wish. She hated not working. It left her with too much time spent alone with her thoughts, dark thoughts that left her confused and depressed; but she'd deal with that when she had to. Right now, if she wasn't going to get her time on the brass pole, she was going to have to go work out. That or get drunk, and it was too soon since her last binge for a drink to taste good.

* * *

Blondie was sweating out the last of the previous night's booze on one of a row of stationary bicycles when the boy toy she'd left handcuffed to his bed blocked her view. "I knew you were brazen but I didn't figure you for plain stupid," Fatso said as he put his hands on his hips and stared at her. He was a little miffed. Maybe she wanted to get caught, a bad girl in distress wanting to be turned good, but even he wasn't that naive. "You do know I own this place?"

It took her a couple of rotations of the pedals to regain her cool. "Ahh, my lay from last night. You clean up pretty good."

"Your lay? Is that all? What about my missing wallet?"

"Did you look under your bed? It was a little soft for me."

"What?"

"Your bed."

"You used a free pass to get in. I checked with the receptionist. I always have a bunch in my wallet."

"I'm hurt. You don't remember giving me one last night?"

She had him there. He couldn't remember if he had or not. It was a standoff, neither could prove the other wrong. He knew it and she knew it. The timer on Blondie's bike beeped and she stopped pedaling. She wiped her face with the towel the gym provided and stared back at him. She'd had a bad day. He was having a bad day, and she actually felt a tinge of guilt over it and even weirder, she had the urge to be nice to him.

She slid off the bike's saddle and stepped up close to him. "It's in the garbage can next to the elevators in your building's lobby. It's probably still there."

"You bitch!"

"Don't call me that. I've had it with being called that," she said and shoved him away.

He landed on his ass with a loud umph! "What? Did you think we'd kiss and make up if you told me?" He got to his feet and his hands were on his hips again. "The lobby has security cameras. You're busted."

She'd given it to him, been stupid. "All right, creep, call the cops."

His hands slid off his hips and went into his pockets. His righteous edge had dulled. He admired her nerve coming into his gym, and her honesty. Nobody else would've done either of those two things. And, he still liked her. That was what stopped him from seeing her another way, that maybe her nerve was simply stupidity and her honesty was really arrogance. But the power of attraction won. "If my wallet is still there I'll drop the whole thing."

* * *

They were silent as they walked through the wet park blocks on their way to Fatso's building, she in her black vinyl raincoat and stripper boots and him in a fresh outfit for clubbing. Now that he had found her he didn't feel like clubbing. He just felt tired. "Do you need money? Is that why you stole it?"

The mist in the air turned to sprinkles and she pulled up her hood. "I was on my way out and it was just there. That's all. Nothing personal."

"Nothing personal," he muttered.

"Don't mutter. It's as bad as whining. If you have something to say, say it."

"Look, I really liked you. We had a good time at Dante's, we slept together, then you ripped me off in the middle of the night. I feel violated."

She stopped walking and pushed her hood aside to look at him. He couldn't be as naive and he sounded. "It wasn't the middle of the night. The sun was coming up." She chuckled. "Check your security tape." She started walking again. "I was amazed you could sleep handcuffed to the bed like that." She stopped and waited for him to catch up. "Actually, I was impressed. Most people drool or look stupid when they're asleep, but you look okay."

When they got to the building, his wallet was still there, and if Fatso had been typical of his breed he would've chalked it up as an interesting experience and never dealt with her again. But he had to learn things the hard way. If he burned his hand on a hot stove, he had to touch it again to make sure it had been the stove that had burned him. Then he'd touch it once more to make real sure, and in a year or two he'd have to have a refresher. Yes, the stove was still hot.

"Do you want to come up?" he asked.

"Is this where we kiss and make up?"

"Maybe, but what's going to stop you from stealing my wallet again if I fall asleep?" he asked, but he was just kidding.

She wasn't. "Nothing. You'll have to hide it where no one can take it unless they wake you. My money has never been stolen. I'll show you where to put it."

Portland Towers

"I was getting headaches until I got the second one," Dinty said, an earphone in each ear with wires leading to the cell phone in his shirtfront pocket. "Now all my calls come in stereo. Like a voice inside my head, right here." He tapped his forehead with his index finger. "If it's my boss, it sounds like the voice of God." Mimicking his boss's deep baritone, he said, "Dinty, public toilet five on the ninth floor has crap smears in it. Get up there with your brush." He scratched the bald spot on the head of the Chihuahua in his lap. "Mr. Orly is like any boss, he's obsessed with smears."

Taking the earphones from his ears, he offered them to the dog. "Here, do you want to listen? I'll call you and I can be the voice of God. 'Stanley, stop shedding on the man's uniform.'" Then the phone rang. The caller ID said it was Mr. Orly. "Oops, speak of the devil. I better take this."

Dinty was one of twelve full-time janitors in the Portland Towers, three cylindrical columns rubbing the gray belly of the overcast sky above. The buildings were state of the art when they were constructed in the 1960s, but now they were concrete monstrosities with leaky plumbing and slow elevators. Dinty loved them. He was a big collector of '60s retro kitsch and being able to live inside a giant monument to that era of snappy colors and chic trinkets was like living in a dream. He didn't mind that the only way he could afford to live there was as the janitor. He felt like a caretaker in a museum, looking after precious artifacts.

He lived in a small basement apartment crowded with his vintage treasures. His most prized was his spoon collection. He had a small spoon from each of the fifty states in the nation, which hung in a cherrywood rack that had an individual slot for each spoon. Dinty's grandmother had willed it to him, knowing he would take good care of it because he agreed with her that the commemorative state spoons you found in today's interstate truck stop gift shops just didn't compare in quality to those from the 60's that made up her collection. It even included a rare spoon from Puerto Rico. She and Dinty used to argue over whether it belonged in the set or not, since Puerto Rico wasn't an actual state but a protectorate. Dinty kept that spoon in the sugar bowl with the sugar cubes. But he still polished it with the others every weekend.

"Hello, Mr. Orly," he said as he answered the phone. Mr. Orly always called him a minute after his lunch hour was over. "I'm on my way."

Mr. Orly was original hardware. He had come with the buildings. He liked Dinty and was grooming him to be his replacement when he finally retired next year. It took a special person to manage three buildings full of so many lives, and sometimes he worried Dinty might not be man enough for it, so he rode him a lot. "Dinty, lunch is over. A resident has a plumbing issue."

"Residence number?" Dinty asked, but he could guess who it was.

"Twenty-three-oh-nine. They requested you."

Twenty-third floor, farthest from the elevator and on the right. Miss Betty Bobcake, the widow who went back to using her maiden name after her husband died. Dinty had been called up there a lot recently. First it was her disposal that had a problem, then it was her washing machine, and then her refrigerator, but that turned out simply to have been unplugged.

"I'll take care of it, sir," he said and hung up. He turned off *Days of our Lives*, set Stanley, a stuffed Chihuahua a former resident had left behind, onto the floor and grabbed his tool bag. At the apartment door he turned off the light and headed upstairs.

Betty Bobcake met him at the door. She was a heavy woman in her forties who resembled a German hausfrau. "Oh, Dinty, you're a lifesaver," she said, sucking on something that smelled like hard candy, apple flavor. Just like the other times, she grabbed his gray uniform sleeve and whisked him inside. "It's this way." She led him through the living room, down a short hall to the bedroom and into the bathroom. "I'm so embarrassed," she said as she released him with a slight push toward the toilet.

It was plugged. "Don't be. It happens to the best of us, Miss Bobcake," he said as he reached for the toilet plunger in his tool bag, though he couldn't remember ever plugging a toilet himself other than the times in grade school when he and his friends did it on purpose.

"Oh, Dinty, I think you can call me Betty by now. Even my husband never had to do this for me."

He doubted that and wondered what had caused her husband's demise as he lowered the plunger into the toilet and plunged. He also took a plunge with Miss Bobcake. "Betty, when did your husband die?"

"Years ago, back when I was thin. Here, I'll show you a photo of us." She left and returned with a silver-framed wedding picture. She held it out for him to look at as he paused his work with the plunger. An old man stood in the center, next to him was his young bride, blonde and willowy. Both were smiling at one another, like grandfather and granddaughter. There were others in the photo, but they were shadows compared to the bride and groom.

"You look very happy," he said and plunged again. "How did he die?"

She held the photo to her bosom, gazing at it quietly. "Oh," she sighed, "I guess I can tell you. He died right here, on this very toilet. Just like Elvis, with his pants around his skinny ankles and a turd bobbing in the bowl."

Dinty stopped plunging and stared at the toilet. It was a typical '60s light blue number. He had no trouble picturing the Rat Pack taking turns filling its bowl and flushing.

"I kept it, you know."

"It?"

"Yes. At first I thought the police had made a mistake when they left it behind. I thought it might be evidence, you know, in case they wanted to check it for poisons, so I kept it in a Tupperware bin in the freezer. But the coroner ruled it a natural death, heart failure on the toilet. They said it was fairly common for older men, something to do with bowel strain."

Dinty knew he was supposed to say something, but instead he pushed down the toilet's handle. The bowl began to fill, but the swirling of the blue water didn't commence, instead it rose slowly toward the rim, and Dinty rushed in with the plunger again but to no avail. It overflowed, a pool of blue on the white tile floor.

"Oh crap!" Dinty cursed. "I'm sorry, Miss Bobcake. This is some clog. I'm gonna have to use the snake."

Betty was still in her own thoughts. "They said I married him for his money because he was so much older than me, but that was never true. He wasn't nearly as famous as Elvis, but he was famous amongst those he worked with, so I kept it even after the police said they didn't need it. I stacked chickens on it, frozen steaks, vegetables, whatever went into the freezer. Eventually it was swallowed up by the frost and it became my hidden secret. Until the other day when the refrigerator was unplugged and everything thawed."

It was now that Dinty took notice of the empty Tupperware container on the counter next to the toilet. It was yellowed and cracked.

"It won't hurt him, will it?" she asked, her voice soft, dreamy.

"Hurt him?"

"Yes, this snake you're going to use."

He put his wet hand on her shoulder to comfort her. "No, Miss Bobcake, he'll be just fine."

Hot Pants

The job was suit-and-tie stuffy, but, still a rebel after years of conformity, Will fought the dress code by wearing Sex Pistols T-shirts under his white button-down shirts and leather thong underwear that made his butt crack itch. He felt the itch was more than worth putting up with considering what it said to the world about who he was. Will was in his thirties and living a dual life. He worked for the DIP Corporation. They manufactured everything from baby formula, sold for consumption outside the U.S. only, to the plastic heel tips on women's shoes.

DIP Corporation was painting itself green for an upcoming consumer advertising campaign, and Will was one of several assigned to buying other companies' pollution credits so that DIP could keep on polluting as usual, but say they weren't. His new job assignment was like being stuck in a McDonald's drive thru on a hot summer day with the car's air-conditioning on the fritz. Some days he would drift off and daydream of a future where he would free himself of his corporate trappings and show up on casual Friday, wearing only his favorite Sid Vicious tank top and red leather thong, and maybe his poolside flip flops.

But until then he would have to content himself with his parallel life as a doorman and bouncer at Dingo's Dive Down Under, a greasy spoon turned nightclub just over the river in the industrial part of town that was being encroached upon by high-rise condo gentrification. Many of his DIP coworkers lived in these condo towers with their concrete walls and spackled ceilings, but Will hadn't run into any of them in line trying to get in to Dingo's and been forced to integrate his day job persona with his night job.

At Dingo's they called him Cow Killer, or just Cow, because he wore a lot of leather, and this was Portland, Oregon, where even a homeless guy on a tricycle was politically correct about wearing animal skins. In winter Cow wore a leather overcoat over leather jeans, and in the summer he wore leather shorts, not lederhosen, but tight black hot pants you'd be more likely to see on Stark Street where the gay bars and saunas were located. But Cow didn't swish that way. He just loved his leather painted on tight so it would creak like a schoolgirl's desk.

It was in these shorts that he bent over to pick up the fake ID of a very nervous yet pretty teen, when he heard a terrible sobbing. It was pure emotion, a young woman wailing in pain. He stood up and looked along the line of eager ravers waiting to get in to the club, but he didn't see anyone who was crying or even looked like she'd been crying. His gaze paused momentarily on one woman who looked familiar, possibly from work, but she was dressed too outlandishly in a pink Pippi Longstocking look for that, and his gaze moved on.

He handed the teenager back her fake ID and let her and her two friends in, then he heard the crying again. It was quieter now, more of a resigned sobbing.

"Do you hear that?" he asked the rocker standing in front of him as he took his proffered ID.

The rocker's expression was blank. His iPod was plugged into his ears, and he could hear nothing over the Megadeath vibrating his synapses. Cow handed back his ID and checked the next person's. "Did you hear that crying a moment ago?" he asked the woman whose ID stated that her bursting cleavage was twenty-three.

"You must be a Sensitive to be able to hear it. That's mother Gaia feeling the pain of global warming. Mankind's pestilence is making her sick."

Cow returned her ID. "Shouldn't that be *human*kind?"

She slipped her drivers license behind her bra with a smile. "Same difference until womankind runs the show."

He let her in ahead of the rocker, who was resigned to waiting. The rocker didn't care. He'd smoked a full bowl of Oregon homegrown before showing up and right then couldn't honestly say he cared about anything.

A new silver Cadillac pulled into the valet parking in front of Dingo's, and the club's owner got out. He was short, portly and bald and only in it for the money. He always said, "Give the kids what they want, they'll come and their parents will pay dearly for it." He'd put this into practice twenty years ago when he opened Portland's first underage dance club. It was a big success and really pulled in the predators. He had to hire guys like Cow to keep them out by checking ID's for anyone over twenty-one.

"How're they hangin'?" the owner asked Cow as he stepped to the head of the line.

Cow unhooked the red velvet rope and lifted it aside. "Close to capacity, Mr. Naval."

"It must be those shorts you're wearing. One of my Stark Street clubs is in a slump. Maybe I should move you over there."

Cow was trying to think of a snappy comeback when he heard the sobbing again. "Do you hear someone crying?"

Mr. Naval grinned. "Oh sure, that's my ex-wife, still in the trunk since our divorce," he said with a conspiratorial wink. "I got a tip the fire marshal is out tonight doing surprise code checks, so don't over pack it, okay?"

"Sure thing. I'll hold the line here," he said, then added, "I was serious about the crying."

"I was serious about my ex-wife," the owner said and disappeared into Dingo's darkness.

At the end of the night when the club stopped serving drinks and closed down, Cow and one of the barmaids, Serena, went to an after-hours speakeasy in Chinatown and ordered "cold tea," a teapot full of beer sold illegally after serving hours. He hadn't heard the crying since soon after the owner's arrival, but asked Serena about it anyway.

"Nope, I didn't hear anything like that, but you can't hear in the club. Once that music gets going it's just thump, thump, thump, like a rhino humping the floor."

On Monday morning, Cow, now Will, was in the DIP office following up on some loose pollution credits he hoped to snatch up to meet his quota for the month so he could slack off for the rest of the week and daydream. One of the girls from the secretarial pool entered his office and set on his desk a couple of sales contracts from last week she'd just finished typing up. "Wow, it's really loud in here. Do you hear that shouting?" she asked, looking about the office for its source.

He didn't hear shouting, but the crying from the club was back. Now he was worried. Maybe he was going crazy with voices inside his head. But then Will's and the secretary's eyes met and they recognized one another.

"You're the bouncer at Dingo's," the secretary said.

"You're Pippi Longstocking."

"My friends and I stayed in line until it stopped moving. I liked your shorts. I dare you to wear them casual Friday."

As he looked her over and liked what he saw, he realized the crying had stopped, and she noticed the shouting had stopped, too. The room was quiet, and Cow broke the silence with his smile. "And what will you wear?"

And she smiled back.

Portland Mud

She was blonde. She was cute. She was sitting alone at the bar. The bartender would come over and say, So and so sitting over there wanted to buy her a drink. She'd say, Fine by me, and order a nice glass of wine, something just above what she would normally pay for. It was a way to try new labels she might not like. Within moments of her sipping her wine, so and so from over there would be at her elbow saying something like, It's not good to drink alone, or, Drinking alone is bad for you, or, I hate drinking alone. She didn't mind drinking alone. It was better than drinking with someone she didn't like. She would shoot the so and so's down and they'd return to somewhere over there. But not the last one.

He pulled out the stool next to her, sat down and said, "My name's Dick. What's yours?"

She smiled at him. He was cute, too. "Well, it's not Dick, I'll tell you that much. Thank you for the wine."

"Oh, it wasn't me who bought it. I just beat the guy who did to the stool. You can pay for your own hangover, that way you won't be able to say I got you drunk before I took advantage of you."

"Is that what you plan to do? Take advantage of me?" She smiled again. She could take care of herself.

"Isn't that what what's his name from over there wanted to do? Isn't that what the wine is for? Isn't that what everyone wants to do? Isn't that what our capitalist society is all about? Getting one over on the next guy so you can make a dime off his sweat? It's not like you came in here, sat down and said to yourself, Wow, I'm going to meet my soul mate tonight, in this place, sitting alone at the bar accepting drinks from strange, lonely men who came here looking for someone who'll let them stick their dick in them."

She smiled at him for the third time. He fell into the bully category: Guys who usually got what they wanted through shock and intimidation. They were exciting and daring at first, but after their newness faded, it became clear their brash manner was a front to hide the little, lost boy who was afraid of getting close because he had intimacy issues stemming from an overbearing mother. They were guys looking for women to mother them so they could act out their rebellious stage again and again with the added benefit of make up sex.

Amused, she sipped her wine. "That was quite the tirade. What else have you got?"

He sighed. "You know you shouldn't drink alone."

"Scraping the bottom of the barrel, huh?"

He turned his charm off. "Yeah. I was bored sitting by my myself and you're cute and I thought I'd give it a go."

Now it was her turn to have fun. "To get your way?"

"Yeah." He ran his finger through the ring of sweat his beer bottle left on the bar top.

"And stick your dick in me?"

He looked up sheepishly, a flicker of hope in his eyes.

"And that stuff about soul mates?"

He looked down at the bar top again, hope gone. "That would be nice, but I'm not sure what it would say about me if I met my soul mate in a bar, half in the bag."

"Would it say more about you if you met them at Starbucks, jacked up on double tall, sickly sweet, non-fat lattes? Or at a job that made you think suicidal thoughts? How about if you met your soul mate in line at the DMV?"

"Everyone has to stand in line at the DMV."

"Exactly," she said and they shared their first pause in their conversation. She sipped her wine. He swigged his beer.

He started it again with, "What do you do?"

She shifted on her stool to re-cross her legs, smiled into his eyes and said, "I'm a hydro-colonic therapist."

He repressed a smile he knew would turn into a grin if he let it. He wanted to say, You're kidding, and had a hard time not saying it.

She touched his knee. "No, let it out. Laugh. You don't want to hold it in and get constipated. I had a friend once who didn't go for days, this was before I was a hydro-colonic therapist, otherwise I could've helped her, and she eventually went to the emergency room. The colon is a very sensitive part of your body. It reacts to all of your emotions."

"And spicy Thai food."

"That, too." And they shared their second pause in their conversation.

She began it again with, "Was your mom an overbearing bitch while you were growing up?"

"No. Why?"

"Just checking a theory." She sipped her wine. "What was she like?"

"She was a great mom. Always there, always helpful. A saint, really."

The bartender came over and said, "So and so over there would like to buy you each a drink."

A man in his 50's raised his wine glass to them and smiled.

They looked at each other and said, "Eew!"

Dick pushed his now empty beer away. "I think that's my cue to leave." He didn't like talking about his mom anyway.

"Me, too. Let's leave together, give him something to fantasize about later."

"I don't know if you're being gross or nice."

She leaned over and picked up her bag from in front of her feet. "Both. Many gross things are nice. Have you ever had a mud bath?"

* * *

Portland wasn't lacking in mud, especially in the rainy fall months, but warm mud had been unavailable unless you were willing to microwave your own. People had tried, but their microwaves hadn't reacted well to the tiny bits of metal they'd failed to remove from the soil they'd dug up from their back yards; Nails, rusty screws, bottle caps. There were a lot of bottle caps, Miller, Bud, Schlitz. A spa had recently opened on the East Side of town supplying Portlanders with all the warm mud they desired. It was named, Portland Mud. They offered private rooms where you could wallow in the mud with your friend or partner for as long as you liked. They rented them by the hour, hourly mud.

Dick and the blond who wasn't named Dick lay facing one another covered head to toe in dark, creamy mud the consistency of chocolate syrup. They shared a tub the size of a twin bed and it even had rubber pillows propping up their heads and shoulders. They didn't speak, but the blond sighed loudly, her hair now filthy. She was enjoying herself, sweating in a vat of wet earth with a cute guy trying to hide his boner in the mud that wasn't quite deep enough. If he wasn't already red from the steam and heat, he'd be blushing.

She winked at him. "Looks like someone enjoys playing in the mud."

He squirmed, trying to push deeper into the tub, but it just made it rise above the surface even more. "I'm sorry, I can't control it."

"I don't mind. I see them all the time at work. Yours is kind of cute. It's wearing a mud had."

"Maybe if we don't talk about it, it'll go away."

"That's what rich people say about the elephant in the room."

"It was pink elephants in my family."

She inhaled deeply, her breasts rising momentarily from the mud, and sighed again. "This is so nice. Have you seen any?"

Staring at her breast, he said, "Pink elephants? No, and I don't plan to."

"That would be the cue for the pink elephants to enter. Do you go out drinking a lot?"

He was relaxing even if his boner wasn't going away. He knew she was right. With a history of pink elephants in his family, going out binge drinking wasn't the smartest thing to be doing, but it was easier to take another swig and put off thinking about, just like no one in the family spoke of the pink elephants that filled his childhood. His mom hadn't been a saint. He just said that because he knew it wasn't cool to talk down your mom to a prospective lay. They'd take it to mean you had mommy issues. He didn't know one guy who didn't, and all his friends seemed to be marrying younger versions of their mothers. It was unlikely he'd ever marry. His mom had been exactly what the sighing, mud covered blond had asked if she was; a controlling bitch.

But there was more to it than that. She had a huge ego which left little room for anyone else, and once she started her cocktails and the pink elephants marched in, there was no room left. She couldn't have always been that way. At some point she must've been different, she must've been nice. His dad had married her and in the beginning they'd been in love. His dad told him that once. She must've slowly metamorphosized into the woman he remembered growing up.

He looked across at the blond, wondering who she might turn into over time. She was sweet and nice and spontaneous now, but as life disappointed, would she become known as the bossy therapist at work? The one, if you were a client, you didn't want to get? This was the true legacy his mother had left him. Not her ego or her alcoholism, but her fear that nobody was what they seemed. The crap you saw them do to others they would eventually do to you, so you might as well prepare for the worse from the beginning. Which left you with no one because everyone was flawed.

He'd had enough of the mud, and his buzz was fading along with his mood. "I'm ready for a shower," he said and sat up, with his last bit of hope wondering if she would offer to soap his back, but doubting she would.

She sensed the change in his mood. The mud always sorted the men from the boys. Those who didn't play in it were trying too hard to be men and didn't really know what it was to be a man, and those who played in it too much, slopped it around and threw it at her, were still boys. She was looking for one who had confidence while laying in his mud. She'd hoped Dick had been her man, that he might rise to the occasion in more ways than he had, but she'd invited him more for not wanting to be alone than his potential as the one she was looking for. She was getting tired of searching and losing faith that she would succeed. She could feel the urge to give in and was afraid she would soon settle for someone like Dick who, she could now see, would with time become a dried out brick. The water that kept him alive would always have to be replenished and the women in his life would be its source. Well, she wasn't going to settle tonight, not for this dick, even if it was cute wearing its mud had.

"You go ahead. I'm going to soak a while longer," she said and closed here eyes, her way of saying goodbye.

Departure, Arrival

I'm sitting in the Dublin Pub with two good friends, Will and Paul. We're drinking pitchers of Henry Weinhard's, waiting for the Fabulous K-Tels to start playing. They're one of our favorite bands in Portland, playing old R&B, like Booker T and the MG's, and a few dated surf tunes. The band brings us three together, strengthens our bonds. It's known for that among our other friends. Wednesday is K-Tels night, a guys' night, the night we three go out and talk guys' talk. It's a different sort of evening than the weekend. We have no dates, no need to entertain, no restrictions. Guys' banter takes care of it all.

Tonight is more intense than usual. I'm leaving tomorrow morning to go to college in Boston. Will and Paul don't have this in common with me. They're staying in Portland. It's very cold outside and it has just snowed. It heightens our moods, increasing my sense of future departure and separation.

The K-Tels are tuning up. They go into a long up-tempo instrumental. The singer introduces the three-by-four linoleum dance floor in front of him. He does this every Wednesday and we laugh each time. The singer is particularly cool. We feel he's one of us. A fourth member of our table who's standing ten feet away. I catch my friends' grins. It's a good night, my last night. The band is hot. We drink more beer and listen.

The band goes into an old surf song, one I played on record for Will and Paul two nights ago. Will looks at me and jokingly makes a hang loose symbol with his hand. I laugh. My feelings of camaraderie intensify. For a moment I wish that I had a few more days, but I will leave in a matter of hours. I'll miss the comfort, the intimacy that friends and familiar places create.

I know I can't stay. If I did the days wouldn't be like tonight. My dissatisfaction with quiet Portland has put a strain on my friendships with Paul and Will that we're each aware of. Tonight is good because the strain is gone. I'm leaving. We all know this and are glad of it, happy that I'm going, but sad that I'm leaving.

* * *

My dad wakes me up. I feel like I never made it to bed. It's 5:30am. My plane leaves in an hour. It'll be close. I almost fall into the shower with my eyes closed. I don't shut them again. As my dad and I drive to the airport, I know I've forgotten things, but won't know what they are until later, later when I need them. I concentrate on what they might be. It's a vent for my tension. I'm nervous about saying goodbye to my dad. We've spent a lot of time together during my past eight months in Portland, time that we missed after my parents divorced a few years back. It makes me sad to leave him. I know he would like Boston.

* * *

The plane lands and taxis to the gate. I stand, walk down the aisle and into the terminal. It's vaguely familiar; I've been here twice before, but need to read the signs to find my way to the baggage room. I'm excited. There are new faces around me which give me the feeling of untapped potential ahead. I feel challenged by a possibility of permanence, something that was missing in Portland.

* * *

I'm in a bohemian bar that reminds me of home. I checked into my dorm room and dumped my bags there earlier. I order a bottle of Bud, familiar no matter where you are. I descend into the bar's basement. A punk band is thrashing. I find out what their name is, the Pajama Slave Dancers. I like their sound, they have personality. I think of the K-Tels and feel that this place will become familiar, too.

Boy or Girl?

The balls clattered across the felt. It was a good break. Skid had his choice of stripes or solids. On the other side of the pool table, Mojo leaned on his stick and sipped his beer. It would be his turn soon. Skid was only good for a run of two or three before he'd flub the shot. The tavern was quiet. They practically had it to themselves.

"Boy or girl?" Mojo asked.

Skid looked up from sighting down the pool stick. "Huh?"

"Which are you and Stephanie hoping for? A boy or a girl?"

"Either," he answered and went back to lining up his shot.

"If it's a boy, you get to raise a little you, and if it's a girl, you're off the hook. It's Stephanie's job to teach all that girl stuff. But wait until she starts dating, then you're in trouble."

Skid flubbed his shot and sunk the cue ball and the eight ball. "She's not pregnant yet, so what's the point?"

"That's exactly it. Now is your chance to influence what gender your kid will be."

Skid sat down at their table by the wall and picked up his beer. Mojo was full of this new age mumbo, always had been.

Skid listened, but not seriously. It would make a good story for Steph. "Go on."

Mojo dug the cue ball out of the table, set it on the felt and lined up a shot. The game was over but he wanted his quarters' worth. "What you do is you choose what sex you want, then think really hard about it as you're doing it, then unload." He took a shot, slamming the six ball in the corner pocket.

"That is messed up on so many levels," Skid said as he unscrewed his stick and put it in its case. He'd had enough pool. "You're as bad as Steph. You know we've been trying for a while. She thought she'd get pregnant right away once we'd decided. Wham bam boom, junior's on his way. We've been doing it like dogs for the past six months and not even a late period. I'm burned out." Skid drank the foam off the top of his pint. "She's reading this book one of her friends gave her, step-by-step on how to get pregnant. We're on a time clock now."

Mojo concentrated on the pool table. "Skid, too much sharing."

"See, that's what I mean. I'll be watching a game or something, you know, chilling out, and she'll come into the room and announce that it's time. Like last night, I'm watching the Pats-Bears game and she came in during the fourth quarter with the score at 7 to 9 and says, 'Honey, it's time.' So there we are, going at it, and I'm watching the game over her shoulder."

Mojo chuckled. "That was a tight game."

"You know what I did?"

Mojo raised his eyebrows.

Skid set his beer down. "I faked it and zipped up, then she said thanks and went back to folding laundry. All I wanted to do was watch the game."

"I didn't know a guy could fake it."

"I didn't either, but I do now." He shook his head, frustrated. "Before Steph I'd slept around a lot and I took my share of chances not wearing a jimmy hat. By the odds alone I should've gotten at least one girl pregnant."

Mojo sunk another ball. "Feel lucky you haven't. Sometimes I'll be sitting doing nothing and out of nowhere it'll hit me, my kid would've been five years old if Gina hadn't had an abortion. Then every kid I see I'll be going, that could've been him, or that could've been her." He set his stick down on the table and picked up his beer. "It messes with your head."

Skid swirled the beer in his glass. "I'm starting to think I've got something wrong with my sperm, like they're just swimming in circles."

"Is that why you faked it?"

"Shit, I don't know." He checked his watch. "I've got to get going in a bit. It'll be time soon, and Steph will be pissed if I miss it."

"Sure, I'm meeting someone later. You can give me a lift. Do we have time for another?" Mojo asked, grinning.

* * *

The two-seater hummed down Broadway. Mojo rubbed his hand on the leather interior. "I still can't get over you driving one of these. This is a nice ride."

"It's fun," Skid said, matter of fact. "Steph is already after me to trade it in on a Chevy Tahoe or some other four-wheel-drive tank."

Mojo pointed ahead. "There it is on the right, that building. You should come in. I want you to meet her."

Skid didn't need to look at his watch. Stephanie would already be mad at him. Might as well put that off. "Sure, why not."

* * *

At the apartment door, Mojo knocked, bouncing on his heels in anticipation. He glanced at his friend. "You'll like her. She's great."

A woman their age answered the door. Smiling, she kissed Mojo in greeting. When she saw Skid, she dropped the smile. Hugging one of her legs was a little boy about four or five. Skid stared at the kid as Mojo made introductions, but he didn't need to be introduced. He'd met her once before at a bar about five years ago.

Holding Hands

Tricia needed her hand held through life. She wasn't exactly afraid of her own shadow, but she was of the hair on men's legs. When she was a young girl, her parents bought her a dog, thinking it would help. When it saw her, it wrapped its paws around her leg for dear life and humped like mad. It had found its mate, the perfect bitch. When she screamed and tried to push the dog off, it bit her. As a grown woman, Tricia had canaries in her apartment, a sexless bird as long as you remain ignorant that it's the males that do the singing to attract a mate, which she happily was. If asked, she'd say it was both male and females that sang and that it had nothing to do with mating. They sang because they liked to, like people who ate chocolate, and when contradicted by a friend, she put her hands over her ears and sang God Bless America, as loud as it took to drown out anything relating to sex.

She'd found a sexless mate for herself, Danny, who had agreed to wait until after they were married to have sex. The small hiccup in this arrangement was that she wanted to wait because sex made her so uncomfortable it brought on panic attacks, and Danny was going along with it because he had thought he was going to die of AIDS and had turned to Christ when it was discovered that the clinic where he had gone to be tested had mismatched his test results with anonymous testee number seventeen, when he was number seventy-one. He felt he was living a borrowed life and in no way was he going to risk it like he had his previous one.

Tricia was okay with kissing because now that they had an agreement she knew it would go nowhere, although they kissed rarely. And Danny was okay with kissing rarely because he didn't like getting all worked up without release. There were things Tricia could do for him, but he sensed suggesting them would not go over well and would make him dirty in her eyes. Waiting was worth it. She was a virgin. She would be safe, disease free and clean, and this gave her greater credibility than himself, unlike the countless girls he'd picked up at the VC on buck night and taken home to screw. Sometimes he didn't bother to take them home but screwed them in his car. It was a tight fit, but two people in the heat of it always made it work. He preferred this. It saved him from the awkwardness in the morning and the drive back to the bar to their car.

Tricia's world was far from his former life. He'd met her in the supermarket, his old habit of picking up girls dying hard, and she even smelled different. She smelled like a virgin. Danny knew that didn't make much sense, he just started associating her smell, the perfume she wore, the scent of her laundry soap on her clothes, her shampoo, with virginity. Bold, Extra Clean, was for virgins. So was Head & Shoulders, and Perfume Ooo La La. He even started using the same brand of detergent, hoping it would wash away some of the memories of his slutty escapades. And when he needed release, he held a T-shirt that smelled of her perfume to his face and thought of the time he'd lost his virginity to a girl he'd just met and now couldn't remember her name. Sometimes he wondered if he'd ever known it. All that didn't matter. In his fantasies he'd renamed her Tricia, Tricia the virgin with a clean past like he had back then when he was thirteen.

In the tense voice she had when the subject of conversation was sex, she asked him about the number of partners he'd been with. He didn't lie to her, but he didn't answer her either. He fobbed her off by saying he was pretty experienced. Later, when he was alone, he laughed about the weakness of his answer. He laughed to keep up his bravado because he was sensing he was in over his head with Tricia and her shyness about sex. It was obviously more than shyness. He'd told her he was experienced because it implied he was a good lover, that he was in demand and that girls came back for more, but the actuality of it was that he was good looking and had that vague charisma that turned girls on, especially girls drinking hard booze at the end of a long, boring week. He knew Tricia's hang-ups would be complex, what girl's wouldn't be who was still a virgin at twenty-four and who wasn't a devout something or other, but he figured he was the guy to help her get over them. They were meant to be, brought together from the opposite ends of the spectrum of sexual experience. She was going to be his ultimate "safe sex." No diseases, no risk of HIV, and no other male partners to compare him to. And he would be her "ultimate" sex, perceived by her however he wanted to spin it.

He held Tricia's hand as they walked down the sidewalk in the rain, protected by his oversized green and yellow Ducks Football umbrella. She loved holding hands. It made her feel connected without feeling threatened. At least until her palm got sweaty, then she would start feeling claustrophobic and would have to free her hand and wipe the dampness from it, like she did now.

"Wipe your hand off," she said with a smile. "I know, it's silly, but indulge me."

He didn't think it was silly. It was one thing to have close contact with someone when he was drunk, and another when he'd had nothing to drink. He smiled back at her as he wiped his palm off on his pant leg. "I like holding hands, but I don't like sweaty palms either."

She took his now dry hand in hers and they continued along the sidewalk. As they walked, he wondered if he had ever had sex while sober, and after giving it a few moments' thought, he realized he hadn't. He was a sober sex virgin, and he smiled at her, knowing that when they finally did it, it would be almost as awkward for him as it was for her.

"What are you smiling at me for?"

He squeezed her hand. "I'll tell you when we get there."

Graffiti

It was on his return visit to the alley where they mugged him that Elmore noticed the graffiti on the wall above his bloodstains, still there on the ground. It hadn't rained since, but it would soon. Portland didn't go long without rain in the fall, and his bloodstains would soon be washed across the cobbles to the street and down the drainage gutter with the fast food wrappers and other detritus. It had been late at night. He had been walking home through downtown from a bar, alone, drunk, and was just a few blocks from his apartment building when a black woman approached him and asked if he was looking for a date. Hookers weren't his thing. He smiled and told her no thanks. But she kept talking and smiling and working him. He didn't care. She was as interesting as the strangers he'd been talking to in the bar. Everyone had a story to tell and their own way of telling it, and he was there to listen to all of them, a visitor exploring the neighborhood he had just moved into. The hooker was laughing at something he said, when he saw the sudden movement out of the corner of his eye and it was over.

* * *

He came to, groggy, lying on his face in the alley.

"Stay down!" Someone shouted from above. It wasn't the hooker. He could smell her perfume as she went through his pockets. The voice belonged to a man. He sounded nervous and scared, like Elmore would be if he weren't sprawled out on the ground, bleeding and half unconscious.

"Don't move, baby. Stay still or he'll hit you again," the hooker said quietly as she took out his keys, then put them back. "Sorry, honey, you were kind of nice."

He lay still like she told him to. There was no point fighting; he'd already lost this round. When they left, he got onto his hands and knees and shook his head like a dog, trying to clear it. His nose was bleeding and his white T-shirt was covered in blood. All he wanted was to get home. He took the alley and avoided the lights of passing cars, embarrassed and ashamed to be seen this way, as if he were the one who'd done wrong and not the friendly hooker and her pimp. When he got to his building, he quietly let himself in and was glad she'd left him his keys. The hooker with the heart of gold, he thought sarcastically.

* * *

He woke the next day with a mixture of being hungover, sore where he'd been hit and depressed from his encounter with the "real" world. The hooker had been black, and though he hadn't seen him, her pimp sounded black and probably was, and Elmore was already having thoughts a white guy wasn't supposed to have. They were probably drug addicts, junkies, robbing people to get their fix. And then he said it, called them the n-word inside his head, and immediately felt there was something wrong with him for saying such a thing even it was only silently.

* * *

The graffiti on the wall in the alley where he'd been mugged had been spray painted on by a clumsy hand, a beginner at this newfound art form. It took Elmore a moment to decipher it, but once he saw it, it was clear. "Niggers." Instead of feeling disgust, he felt relieved that he wasn't alone. Someone else had been there before him and had lain bleeding on the ground. Their anger had been pushed past its limit and they, too, had said what they weren't supposed to say.

Then it came to him. The hooker and pimp would probably be back tonight. He could wait for them and catch them, at least find out sober what they looked like. He glanced at his blood on the ground and touched the bruised skin around his eye and nose where he'd been hit. But first he would have to decide if he would let that word out of him, say it aloud to their black faces, or if he would be better off keeping it inside and only saying it to himself silently in his head.

* * *

Elmore found a spot between two dumpsters halfway down the alley. He angled them so that he could hide behind them and not be seen, and settled in to wait. He didn't have to wait long. In the glow from the street light at the end of the alley he saw the hooker round the corner and enter the alley. She wasn't as good looking as he remembered, but he was sober now. She was followed by a guy not unlike himself last night. They came toward Elmore's hiding place until they were directly in front of his dumpsters, then moved against the wall. The john gave her some money and she unbuckled his pants and squatted in front of him. They were so close he could hear the saliva in her mouth envelop him.

The mist in the air was changing to rain as another guy entered the alley from the same end as they had. Again, the guy wasn't much different than Elmore, white, mid-twenties. Elmore figured him for the john's friend, and they were both going to use the hooker's services. But he wasn't a friend. He went up to the john, who'd opened his eyes at the sound of footsteps, and struck him in the head. Already leaning against the wall, the john's head hit the bricks.

"Pass over your wallet," the pimp said. Elmore recognized the voice. It was the same guy, and he did sound black. "And I'll take that watch, too."

"What the fuck?" the john asked angrily. "Ouch!" he snapped, looking down at the hooker staring up at him.

"Make it fast. She's getting tired of keeping your dick warm."

The john did as he was told. The pimp hit him again anyway and he fell down sideways along the wall. The hooker stood up glared at her pimp. "You took your time. The guy almost came in my mouth. You know I hate that."

The pimp laughed a high, nervous laugh as he took the money and credit cards and threw the empty wallet at the john. "He won't be sticking his dick in anything for a long time."

Elmore watched them leave and he stayed in his hiding place until the john picked up his wallet, cursed and left. The hooker and pimp would pull their scam again, and he would continue to watch, unable to do anything, not even call them names inside his head.

Naked Fridays

Duane was in jail waiting to be transferred to the state psych hospital in Salem for a 24-hour observation and evaluation period. He didn't blame them. He'd been arrested standing naked on a milk crate in Pioneer Courthouse Square. The night before, while his wife and two-year-old were asleep, he was up late in the glare of the kitchen sitting in the eating nook finishing the details of a big contract that was to be signed in the morning. The house was silent, except for the hum of the refrigerator, when a warm breeze fluttered the sheets of paper in front of him off the table. Duane looked up to see what was amiss and standing next to him was a man, not an ordinary man, but an extraordinary man if he was a man at all. He wore a long, dingy brown robe that had seen better days and from his back sprouted a pair of giant vulture wings as wide as he was tall. Their feathers glistened in the brightness of the kitchen as if he had just come in from the rain. He announced himself to be the angel Gabriel and took the chair next to Duane, saying they needed to talk. The Lord was happy with Casual Fridays, he said, but like many aspects of modern society, it was too watered down. It would please the Lord for His creations to go about on Fridays as they came into this world, and if all do this and the Lord is pleased, He may bring back the Garden of Eden for all to live in.

Duane woke fuzzy headed in the middle of the night at the kitchen table with his head on tomorrow's contract and a small puddle of drool where the signers were supposed to date their signatures. He packed up all the paperwork in his briefcase and went to bed. In the morning he kissed his wife and baby boy goodbye and left for the office downtown.

It was after the signing of the big contract when all the participants were standing around congratulating each other like one big winning sports team, that Duane remembered the angel Gabriel's visit and began to feel restricted by the knot in his necktie. It was his Casual Friday tie, navy blue with small, yellow, smiling fishes. At first he only planned to loosen it, but that wasn't enough, so he took it off. The others in the room didn't mind. The deal had been signed, they'd all make a lot of money and thought they'd gotten the better of the other and could relax now. But then, thinking of the return of the Garden of Eden, he slipped off his suit jacket and unbuttoned his shirt collar. Contracts wouldn't be important there, he thought as he continued to unbutton his shirt. Who needs contracts when you're naked?

When his shirt was open to his navel, his secretary was so confused she had trouble speaking. Why was her boss disrobing? He barely had a sense of humor, so what kind of joke was this? "Sir, what are you doing?"

"An amazing thing happened to me last night," he told everyone as he slipped out of his shirt, folded it and placed it next to his briefcase on the conference table everyone was standing around. "The angel Gabriel came to me and declared me to be a prophet in a long line of prophets. There was Abraham, Moses, Mohammad, and now me, Prophet Duane. Casual Friday's are not enough. He said the Garden of Eden will return if we all go naked on Fridays." He undid his belt and trousers and stepped out of them, then folded them and put them on top of his shirt. His red candy cane striped boxers came off next.

His audience was flabbergasted into silence as he stood in front of them in his dark blue socks that were bunched around his ankles and his black wingtips. He looked down at his freshly polished shoes. He'd stopped at the stand in the building's lobby on the way up this morning, and the ancient black man had given him a spit shine, something he didn't do for just anyone, but only for his regulars. At least that was what he said.

"Gabriel probably meant shoes and socks, too. Crap, I hate having cold feet." But he crouched down and began unlacing them anyway.

"But sir, what about all the broken glass outside? Surely he didn't intend for you to walk on that." His secretary tried to reason with him, hoping that if she could get him to keep his shoes on, the tide could be turned, and he might put the rest of his clothes back on, and this entire incident of Duane going naked could be laughed off. He'd be known as the boss that was really smart, but tightly wound. In fact it might even enhance his reputation for being brainy. Everyone knew geniuses were eccentric.

But Duane was a step ahead of her. He liked her logic because he liked his shoes but he knew it was faulty. "I guess we'll all build up calluses on our feet like the Aborigines in Australia." And off came the shoes and socks. He set them on top of his boxers, then picked up his pile of clothes and dropped them in his briefcase and latched it shut. He looked about the room and smiled at the others, and they looked on in mild horror as they saw for the first time what fragile tendrils tethered each of them to reality.

His secretary thought of herding everyone out, but it was too late for that. Her boss had always been so very ordinary. He was always on time, easy to work for; his feet even stunk now that his shoes were off. How could this ordinary guy with smelly feet nose-dive at the peak of his career? She closed her eyes for a moment. No one would be laughing this one off, and she would to have to break in a new boss. Damn.

"Duane," she said softly. "I'm going to call your wife. Maybe you should take the afternoon off and get some rest." His skin was very pale. It hadn't seen sunlight since he was in college. "Maybe work on your tan if you're going to be naked on Fridays."

He nodded his head and smiled some more. "That's a good idea. I might even go to a tanning booth. But first I need to pass on the word of our Lord. Gabriel said it wasn't for me alone to go without clothes. I must convince everyone else to free themselves of their trappings so they too can reach for the prize of Eden." Saying that, he picked up his briefcase and left for Pioneer Courthouse Square.

His wife tried to post bail, but the desk sergeant at the downtown precinct station said it wouldn't be until after her husband's psych evaluation that they would consider releasing him. Her husband had gone along with the arrest peaceably; it was his violent reaction to putting on the orange jail clothes that put them on to him. The police were convinced he was having a psychotic episode brought on by PCP use, or as it's known on the street, angel dust. She told them Duane wasn't a drug user, but the sergeant blew her off, saying maybe someone at the office had a grudge and slipped something in his coffee. Is he banging his secretary? the sergeant asked. He always asked the wives that. It shut them right up.

They released him Sunday morning with a handful of citations: indecent exposure, unlawful gathering, loitering, etc., and he rode home with his wife wearing clothes she had brought for him. On Monday he went to work like nothing ever happened. His co-workers asked him how he was and if he'd gotten a good rest, and he smiled yes and thanked them for asking. They didn't know about his weekend in jail and upcoming court date. But the week went smoothly and even his secretary began to forget what his feet smelled like.

But on Friday morning his wife called in sick for him after she found him sitting stark naked at the kitchen table and asked her over his bowl of cereal if she thought flip-flops were clothes. Across from him their naked two-year-old son was crying because he'd just crapped in his highchair. Diapers obviously were clothes.

"Honey, you need help," his wife told him. "You need to go see someone. They have medications for these sort of ..." she wanted to say, breakdowns, but softened it by saying, "things."

He put his spoon down in his bowl. "But dear, the angel Gabriel can't just be ignored."

"Fuck the angel Gabriel! He's not the one running around naked on Casual Fridays." She lost it. She'd married a boring man because she wanted a boring man, someone who lived a routine of off to work at seven and back for dinner by six. She had a baby to care for all day and that was enough.

He stood up and took the keys from the counter. "With time, you will see," he said and went out to the garage. She heard the garage door open as the minivan started, and he was gone. She stared at the bowl he left on the kitchen table. Even naked he didn't clean up after himself.

Duane found a place to leave the van downtown near the park blocks next to Portland State University. He hoped younger minds would be more receptive to his message, and they were. He stood on his red milk crate and started talking about pleasing God with one's nakedness. "God loves nakedness. It's the way

He brings us into this world. It pleases Him to see our skin in all its variety of shades, but we must no longer cover up our most exciting places. It would please God even more to see them, too."

Soon a small crowd gathered. It was warm and sunny out, and a few guys playing Frisbee had stopped to listen. They had their shirts off, and Duane was hoping it was due to something he'd said when two attractive hippy chicks high on grass pealed off their pink and yellow tank tops. After that, the size of the crowd grew substantially. They weren't naked, but they were at least listening, which was more than his wife did. By the time campus security showed up to enforce Satan's decency laws, Duane had skedaddled to his minivan and was on his way back to the suburbs. He had preached naked, convinced two women to go topless, and not gotten arrested. All in all, he considered the day a success.

The following Friday was also a success, and word got out on campus to go check out the naked preacher and the hippie chicks on Fridays in the park blocks. The crowd was bigger and more people went topless. It was like spring break in Cancun had come to Portland, and then the two cute hippie chicks got really high on grass and decided to go completely naked. Duane's eyes welled up with tears at the sight of them peeling off their panties. He now had two followers, attested to by their nakedness, and it certainly helped his cause that they were hot.

He raised his arms high toward the sky. "Hallelujah! There is only nakedness, and nakedness pleases God! Show Him your nipples! Show Him your pee pee!" he shouted, shaking his dingaling. This was in August and the crowds grew with the temperatures. The local media began calling it the revival of the Summer of Love. September was dry and warm too, but then came October and the rain. The temperature dropped and so did attendance. Nobody wanted to stand in the rain naked and cold. When Duane was finally arrested again, he had pneumonia and was hospitalized. His wife didn't come to visit, but he didn't care. She wore clothes to bed even on Fridays. It was while he was half out of his gourd on high grade cold medicine that the angel Gabriel came to him again.

He stood at the foot of his bed with his black wings folded high up on his back. "You've done well, Prophet Duane. You have been naked every Friday and have led others to follow you. The Lord is pleased. When you wake tomorrow, paradise shall return."

The next morning when he woke he felt much better. But of course he would feel better, he thought. Pneumonia wouldn't exist in paradise. In fact, he guessed a lot of people would be checking out of the hospital today.

But when the nurse came in and went through the usual morning ritual of taking his temperature and asking him how he felt, her ordinariness troubled him.

"Is anything," he paused to choose the most appropriate word, "different today?"

The nurse smiled at him and rubbed his arm. "Oh yes, there are big things in store for you."

Duane flooded with relief. "There are?"

"Yes, you're going home today."

"You mean Heaven?"

His eyes told her his story. The nurse rubbed his arm some more. "I'm sorry, honey. We'll see about getting you into a shelter."

He was discharged that Thursday afternoon wearing donated clothes that hung from his skinny frame and donated red sneakers that were something a teenager would choose to wear. He went through the set of pneumatic doors and out onto the sidewalk. It was cold and raining and he was glad of the warmth of the clothes and didn't look forward to tomorrow when he would have to preach naked again. He looked around at the water-soaked concrete buildings and sighed. The angel told him he'd wake to paradise, but it was the same dreary place as when he went into the hospital. He shook his head and looked down at his sneakers being pelted by the rain. Had the angel lied? Been wrong? Had something happened to change the Lord's mind? This couldn't be paradise.

Duane shook his head again and then it came to him. How far south could he get before midnight when he would have to take off his clothes? It would be warmer down south, and if he kept going it would be warm all the time. He started walking toward the freeway entrance for I-5 south. If he got lucky, he might get a ride with someone who wouldn't mind him stripping in their car halfway to San Francisco. He'd have to explain it to them first, though, about how it was the Lord's wish that he go naked on Fridays and that it had just passed midnight. They might even drive naked with him if he explained it well enough.

Red Box

It was my first day in the court-sentenced anger management class. My community service picking up roadside garbage started next week. I sat toward the back, by the windows, and prepared to be bored. It was high school all over again except the room was filled with people of all ages, a cross-section of Portland, some rich, some poor, some probably homeless. It was a big turnout and the floor mounted desks were all taken. A lanky, bearded guy came into the room pushing glasses up the bridge of his nose and declared himself the instructor. He was going to instruct us in how to manage our anger. He went up and down the aisles of desks handing out ruled notebook paper and cheap ballpoint pens.

When he'd finished that, he returned to the front of the classroom and with his hands on his hips, stood before us. "Write down why you're here. And say something more than because you have to be. I've heard all the smart ass answers so why not be the first group to skip that? When you're done, we're going to read these aloud to the group."

I was there because I'd pled no contest, and the judge said I seemed like a man in need of some help and sentenced me to forty hours of community service and this class. I was there because I'd lost it. I'd lost my control, my sense of reality. I was there because just for a moment I couldn't take it anymore and stopped caring. My father was sick with cancer and it was taking him away. Not all at once, but slowly and humiliatingly.

The stress from my father's cancer brought to the surface the emotional strain in the family. I had two sisters, but since my Dad's diagnosis, felt like I only had one, the younger one, Tricia. The older one, Cynthis, was collateral damage from the cancer. Dogs carry parasites in their intestines all the time. In a sense, dogs always have worms, but stress or an injury can bring on an outbreak where they show up in their stool. That's when you give them the dewormer. Cynthia's mental issues had stayed within the social norm waiting for the right stress to rage into the open. Dad's cancer did that. She was the take charge type who never finished anything because she would get sidetracked taking charge of the next project. She tried to make Dad's illness all about her. That somehow the attention that was going to him should first be routed through her, so she, like a casino, could take her cut. She loved bringing soup to bedridden people, it made her feel flush with the power of life and death, and if you could control the life of another, how could you ever die? There wasn't a dewormer for Cynthia.

I doodled on the corner of the notebook paper. A half year or so before Dad was diagnosed with stage four cancer, I moved from Boston, where he lived, to Portland, Oregon. When I left, he was getting around town on his bicycle and looked ten years younger than his sixty-five. Except for when I went to college, I had always lived in the same town as him, and was moving to get out on my own and think for myself. It wasn't that I was dependent on him, but that it was too easy to fall into a role of the good son asking Dad for advice on any half-important decision I had to make. I'd been taking the easy route, relying on others to make decisions and then getting angry at them when things didn't work out. I wanted to go where that wasn't an option, where I'd make my own decisions, but really, make my own mistakes and have no one but myself to blame for them. I didn't know then that that had more to do with where you lived in your head than which town you called home.

Eight months after I moved, I was back in Boston with Tricia packing up our father's things so we could put his rambling house on the market and move him to Portland where we could care for him. Cynthia was a no-show. When I arrived at his house after driving across country, Dad answered the door looking drawn and pale, with legs so swollen with edema they made his khaki trousers tight down to his knees. He had tumors hindering his lymph nodes from doing their job of turning waste fluid into urine and that was why his legs were so swollen. After he moved and got settled in Portland, I found myself in complicated territory, having a sick dad I wanted to be independent of, but who now needed my help getting to and from his chemo appointments and doing small things, like going to the grocery store.

I felt a lot of anger toward my parents, going back to their separation when I was fifteen. Mom started dating and drinking heavily and staying out late, and Dad moved out and was hardly heard from. They were busy acting like teenagers again while my sheltered life fell apart. The ones who were supposed to be my guides couldn't be counted on and couldn't be trusted. They'd hurt me and let me down. Then I discovered drinking. The first time I got drunk it took three malt liquors and I never felt so good in my life. Having no home life, no parents, and living on tubs of store bought potato salad no longer bothered me. I could put up with all that as long as I could get a buzz on after school.

That first can of Schlitz put me on a long arc of emotional self-destruction that didn't hit ground until I finally quit drinking at forty.

If asked, I wouldn't admit to still being angry at my parents for their behavior back then— how embarrassing to be emotionally hung up on something that took place so many years ago—but I'd be lying to the person who asked and to myself. That anger, my parents' inability to be parents and their selfish, self-absorbed return to teendom, changed the course of my life completely. My anger became like the background radiation left over from the Big Bang. It was everywhere, to the point that it was natural and I no longer noticed it.

On a recent afternoon when I was visiting Dad's apartment, he brought up that period of time when he and Mom separated and then divorced. He said he felt he'd let me down, that he could've been a better father. I could tell it had been weighing on him. Here he was, a man experiencing the close of his life who could only ingest sufficient calories by drinking eight small bottles of Ensure a day, and most days he couldn't even get them all down, was now, in his own way, asking his adult son for forgiveness for something that happened thirty years ago.

What he said stuck with me, and over-night I felt guilty for still being angry at him. The next day I said to him, "You know what we talked about yesterday, that stuff you said about when you and Mom divorced? You shouldn't let that weigh on you." I said it quick because I was going to choke up with emotion and didn't want to cry sitting there as Dad lay in bed, too tired to get up. "It was a difficult time for everyone, and even though it implies blame, I forgive you." If I could forgive my dad, maybe I could let go of that anger and stop carrying it around, cleanse that the background radiation from my life.

The anger didn't go away; if anything, it was more exposed than ever. I was raw and vulnerable because I'd acknowledged the anger and some of its cause, and that afternoon as I checked the selection of movies in the Red Box in front of the grocery store, looking for some escape—action, comedy, anything to stop dwelling on the down side of life, a woman in her twenties stepped up behind me and asked if she could cut in to return the movie she held in her hand. I smiled, said sure and stepped aside.

Before she'd finished, a guy I assumed was her boyfriend came alongside her. "Let's rent something for tonight."

The young woman smiled over her shoulder at me and said, "Sure," to her boyfriend, who started flipping through the movies like I'd been doing moments before.

"Excuse me," I said, feeling my anger rise, "but I was ahead of you."

"I'm with her," he said over his shoulder.

"Yea, but I was ahead of her."

The guy turned around to face me. "Dude, what is your problem? You're there, we're here. How could you be ahead of us?"

I looked to the woman to explain it to him, but all she said was that they'd make it quick. Something slipped loose in me, like a boat breaking free in a Willamette current after a strong rain. "You've got to be kidding me. I let you in front of me and this is what you do?"

"Hey, man, back off," the guy said and pushed me in the chest with both hands.

He shouldn't have touched me. It was the key in the lock to a couple of bad decades. I suddenly saw someone I could be mad at, someone I could vent my pent up anger at, anger at my parents' divorce thirty years ago, anger at my dad, at his cancer and the guilt I felt for being angry at him. I balled my hand into a fist around that accumulated bullshit and brought it around in a wide arc into the side of the guy's head. He stumbled sideways, and I filled my left fist with hate and rage and slammed it into his guts. He buckled over, struggling to breathe. I shoved him away and he fell to the ground. When he started to get up, I screamed at him to stay down. "If you get up, I'll hit you again and I won't stop."

He looked up at me, saw my eyes and knew I wasn't kidding, that I'd snapped. The woman had been fast with her cell phone, dialing 911, and the cops showed up with me still standing over him laying prostrate in the parking lot. When they put me in the back of the squad car, I felt foolish and ashamed of what I'd just done, but somehow powerful, like I'd stood up for myself for the first time. I felt that now as I stopped doodling on the notebook paper and started writing about why I was there. When I'd filled the first sheet, I raised my hand and asked for another.

The Curse

Teresa, Tracy, names from her past when she had little say in what people called her or how they saw her. Her mother had been in charge of that. She dressed her in pink cotton frocks with dark pink flowers and bows on her sleeves and scolded her when she fell and got dirt on her hem. Her mother named her after Mother Teresa, but when Mother Teresa died and the Vatican put her on the fast track to sainthood, she started calling her Tracy.

When Tracy turned eighteen, she went down to Portland City Hall and legally changed her name to Sister Moonbeam. She hadn't been going by Tracy since she moved out of her mother's house at thirteen, but she savored the formality of killing the last thing other than life her mother had given her. She'd never been a Teresa, a Tracy, a perfect little daughter whose sole purpose was to be one of her mother's accessories.

Thoughts of this flashed through her mind as she said into her cell phone, "You did what?"

Her own daughter, Sunshine, was a freshman at Portland State University, and had just turned eighteen. "You don't even need to go to City Hall. You can practically do it online," her daughter said. "You just fill out a form, la-di-da. So guess what you can now address me as?"

Sister Moonbeam had had this same conversation with her own mother years ago, but now the impossible, the hateful had happened. She'd become her mother. "How could you? I gave you that name. You were a ray of light in a very dark time."

"The Reagan Administration wasn't exactly a dark time, mother," Sunshine said, then cleared her throat to make her announcement. "No more Sunshine for you. From now on you may refer to me as Teresa, or Tracy if you're feeling maternal, which you and I both know is unlikely, so you might as well stick with Teresa."

"Sunny, how could you? That of all names."

"I could say the same thing, Mother. Nana never got over you naming yourself Sister Moonbeam." There was a heavy silence on the line as both women seethed with old grudges, then the new Teresa said, "I always thought that if I called you Mother or Mom enough times you would start acting like one. That was pretty naive of me, but that was Sunny thinking, not Teresa. And Teresa says, goodbye, Mom, gotta go. I just wanted to let you know the exciting news." And the signal went dead.

Moonbeam snapped her phone shut and threw it in her bag. She was dressed as if it were night instead of a sunny afternoon. She wore a dress of black gauze with knots tied down the front of it, exposing her pale bluish skin from her clavicle to her studded, pierced and chained bellybutton. It was difficult being a Goth in summer. Her motivation flagged and the edge was off her sarcasm, and now her daughter was ecstatic being the preppy twit Moonbeam's own mother had always wanted Moonbeam to be.

When the light changed and the sign said walk, she stormed across the crosswalk and along the half-block to where she'd parked her car, a lime green VW bug. It was one of the new ones and when she tossed her oversized bag onto the passenger seat she almost snapped off the plastic flower holder on the dash and the dried black rose it held.

She started the car, and the whole way home she thought of the pentagram painted on the attic floor and the black candles she would light. She knew just how to get back at her daughter. The little bitch wants to be Princess Teresa, Moonbeam thought with a scowl, always with the pink, always with the ribbons and bows and lace. She wanted a perfect life behind a white picket fence with her legs spread for a plastic Ken doll. Well, Moonbeam knew how to make mold grow on that white fence.

* * *

Sunny was on the fast track to being a first lady of the suburbs: large home, three car garage, BMW SUV, plenty of time to shop and a boy who would pay for it all. Throughout her years at Lincoln High School, she had well-heeled boyfriends who lived in the West Hills overlooking downtown, but in her freshmen year at Portland State, she cut from the herd a real keeper, a trust baby who would come into his money at twenty-one. The big plus was that he had no trustees or parents to tell him what to do or what not to spend it on. She would do that. His name was Andrew, but he went by Drew, and was good looking in a moneyed, clean-cut, new century, preppy sort of way, and Sunny was in love with him. It helped that he would soon be loaded, but she really did love him. To her he was inseparable from his money. He embodied it, and she'd been in love with old-money guys ever since she found out they existed.

Under the sheets, working away toward her goal, Sunny was confronted with a dilemma: Continue fellation, or stop and say something? At what point do you give up on a limp penis? In all the handjobs and hummers she'd given she'd never dealt with this problem before, and it sure wasn't normal for an eighteen-year-old guy not to go boing just at the prospect of oral sex. She checked her Gucci watch, a high school graduation gift, and decided to give it another thirty seconds when it came to her what was happening.

She sat up with a loud lip pop. "Oh my God," she shouted, the sheet still over her head like Casper the friendly ghost.

Drew flushed with anxiety. "What is it?"

She pulled the sheet from her face. "My witch of a mother has stolen your boner."

Drew glanced down. His penis was still there. "What are you going on about?"

"I must've really made her angry with that prank about changing my name. She's put the curse of the limp dick on you. It's one of her favorites."

"A curse?" Drew didn't know whether to laugh or to leave. He thought she'd found lipstick on him from the previous girl's administrations. Sunny wasn't the only one lured by a wealthy penis. "How long does it last?" he asked, humoring her.

"Forever, or until the curse is broken. I'll need to get some help."

"Now you're talking," Drew said with a grin. "How about your friend, Angie?"

"No silly, not another girl," she said, squeezing him. "I mean a witch at least as powerful as my mom."

"Your mom's a witch?" But his question went unanswered. "I always thought you meant bitch when you said that."

"Oh, she's that, too."

* * *

The house loomed at the top of the dead-end street like a scarecrow over a field of stripped corn stalks. It was the oldest house in a neighborhood built on land that was a farm a hundred years ago. Over the years the farm was sold, parcel by parcel, until the fields were gone and the suburb had surrounded the house. Sunny climbed the creaking old steps to the front porch and rang the cow bell that hung next to the stained glass door depicting the crucifixion. Her mother had brought her here many times when she was a little girl and the bloody man on the cross had always frightened her.

The outline of an old woman could be seen moving behind the stained glass, and narrow eyes appeared in the clear glass above Jesus. Though she wasn't a relative, Sunny had always called her Aunt Zinnia. She'd been a sort of surrogate mother to Sunny's mother until they'd had a falling out a few years back. Sunny was counting on that falling out to recruit her help against her mother's curse.

"Sunny, what a pleasant surprise," Aunt Zinnia said as she opened the door. "I thought you might be the UPS man bringing me my toad hearts and eye of newt."

"There's no such thing," Sunny said as they gave each other a short hug.

"What do you mean? TV witches swear by the stuff. Come in. I'll fix us some tea."

When they were settled in the musty sitting room where everything was covered in drab colored doilies, Sunny brought up her problem. "It's my mother. She's done something horrible."

"That's your mother. She does things. Sometimes things she shouldn't. It's always been her way. You can either accept it or reject it," Zinnia said, and it was clear which she had done.

Sunny set her tea cup down on its matching saucer, thinking that the last time she'd drunk out of real china had been here as a little girl, except that her mother had been there too. "When my mother was my age, she complained a lot about her mother, right?"

"Oh, all the time. They wanted very different things."

"Did she ever say anything like, 'God, my mother is such a bitch, if I ever do anything like that, shoot me?'"

"More than once."

Sunny smiled. "Then get your gun. It's time for you to shoot her."

"Has it come to matricide so soon? I doubt that old gun of my husband's, God rest his soul, still works. I never did find where he kept the bullets. Tell me, what is it she's done? Maybe we can fix it without being so direct."

Sunny picked up her tea and sipped. "She's stolen my boyfriend's erection."

Aunt Zinnia laughed, but stopped when she realized Sunny's seriousness. "I always said she overused that one. Your mother really does have a rather narrow portfolio of spells," Aunt Zinnia said, exaggerating her calm to make up for her laughter. "You're in luck. I know a potion that can easily break that one. Let me go gather the ingredients."

In the upstairs bathroom amongst a dozen other prescription bottles, she found her husband's bottle of Viagra, checked the date and poured a few into her palm. Using the heel of her shoe, she crushed them into a powder on the linoleum, then swept the blue dust into a Ziploc bag and returned downstairs to the sitting room.

She held the bag out to Sunny. "Here you go, sweetie, one teaspoon of this a half hour before amorous activity and the two of you will be just fine."

* * *

When Sunny met up with Drew early that afternoon at her studio apartment, she made him a mug of tea and put in double the dose Aunt Zinnia told her to use. Then she realized Aunt Zinnia would've anticipated her putting in twice the dose and probably told her only half of what to put in, so she quadrupled the dose. When she added the milk, tiny blue specs floated on top. She stirred and stirred, but they wouldn't go away. Oh well, she thought, she would risk it. Drew rarely looked at what he put in his mouth anyway.

He was gazing out the window as the evening shadows grew long when Sunny stepped out of the kitchenette. "Here, honey, have a cup of tea and relax," she said as she handed him the mug and guided him over to her futon couch. Once seated he took a hesitant sip. "Tastes good, doesn't it," she said, being a strong believer in the power of suggestion.

"No, not really. What are these blue flecks floating on top?"

"A new sweetener I'm trying. You really should drink more tea instead of coffee. It's full of antioxidants. They'll clean your system of free radicals," she said, then wondered if the anti-oxidants might damage the potion's effect.

"The only free radicals I know are—"

"Shhh, drink your tea before it gets cold," Sunny said as sweetly as she could.

Drew stared at her over the rim of the mug. He didn't like tea, but he didn't want to fight over not drinking his tea like she was his mother. He was recently feeling claustrophobic around her, and she was doing a lot of smothering, too. What he really wanted was to get outside and catch the last of the sun before it slipped behind the West Hills. He looked into the mug, then gulped it down to get it over with. He set the mug on the coffee table with one hand and wiped his mouth with the back of the other. "There, all done. Are you happy?"

She picked up the mug with both hands, checked that there wasn't any sludge in the bottom and smiled at him. "I'll just go rinse this out," she said and carried it behind the curtain into the kitchenette. She took her time at the sink, killing a few of the thirty minutes Aunt Zinnia said it would take. When she returned to her living room/bedroom, Drew was back at the window. He was sitting on the sill, the window pulled up as far as it would go, staring down at the café across the street with its sidewalk tables. They were filling up with after work drinkers, and it looked like fun to him.

When he heard her come back, he asked, “So what’s the plan for tonight, Sunny? Or do I need to call you Tracy?”

“I have no intention of changing my name like she did. Sister Moonbeam, could she be more corny? I just said that to her to her to piss her off.”

“Why?” He’d met her mom and thought she was pretty cool, an anti-establishment throwback.

“You wouldn’t understand.”

He turned his back to her to look at the café “No, I guess I wouldn’t.”

“I didn’t mean it like that.”

He knew she didn’t, but he was realizing that conversation with Sunny was like verbal combat, and it helped to get her off balance if he were to occasionally get what he wanted. “Let’s go across the street and have a beer.”

Sunny rolled her eyes. A beer to Drew meant half a dozen which would lead to another half a dozen down the street clubbing in Old Town, and that didn’t fit her plans for the evening at all. “I thought we’d stay in and watch some TV. My shows are on tonight.”

“Sunny, we did that last night.” They’d been doing that more and more. Next she’d want to study together. “Come on, we’re going out,” he said, standing up.

She went to him and put her arms around his waist and nuzzled his neck. “But, honey, I can think of something else we can do.” Her hands drifted to his belt buckle and started unbuckling it. She pulled him toward the futon couch. “Drew, I know you want to.”

It was clear from the bulge in his boxers that Aunt Zinnia's dead husband's Viagra wasn't past its due date. Sunny pushed him back onto the futon and climbed up on top of him. Hiking her skirt, she was happy she'd beaten her mother at her own game and gotten her boyfriend's erection back. When they finished, Drew got up to use the bathroom, and Sunny pulled her skirt back in place and grabbed the TV remote. Drew loved football, and a game would definitely keep him in. She tried to find a U of O Ducks football game, hopping from channel to channel, but wasn't having any luck. It didn't help that it wasn't football season. She didn't keep track of those things.

Drew came back into the room and stood at the end of the futon with a big grin on his face. Sunny looked up at him, glad she'd made him happy. "What is it?" she asked.

He adjusted the waist of his jeans. "This is some boner I got. It won't go away."

She was confused. "It won't? But we just—"

"I know, pretty cool, huh?" He grabbed his crotch to feel it still there. "Wow."

"Don't be crass."

He let go and fluffed out his jeans. "Does it show much?"

"Sort of."

"This is so cool," he said. "I really gotta go out now."

She took his hand and pulled him toward the couch. "Maybe if you sat down and watched some TV it would go away."

He pulled his hand free. "What is it with you and the TV? Fuck the TV." He grabbed his jacket off the chair by the door. He wasn't going to waste a magic boner like this one watching TV. "I'm going and I won't be staying here tonight." He slammed the door on his way out, the noise ringing off the walls of the small apartment.

* * *

"Hello?" Moonbeam answered her phone on the first ring. She was expecting a call from a friend who wanted help casting an impotence spell on the president, and Moonbeam wanted to talk her out of it because she was worried a sexually frustrated president would be a dangerous president.

"First you stole my boyfriend's penis, then you make me give him a potion to break your curse. Now he's left me and is out there on his own exploring the night with a super boner that won't quit and there's no telling where he'll stick it, you bitch."

"Two calls from my daughter in the same week, I'm blessed," she said sarcastically, not understanding at all what her daughter was angry about. "Sunny, I didn't do anything to your boyfriend."

"I don't believe you," Sunny shouted. "I'll never believe you."

Once again Sunny's mom had a weird feeling of coming full circle. She could remember saying the same thing to her own mother years ago. It made her sad, but she was becoming resigned to the ironic twists of life. Sunny should've been her mother's daughter, but all that pink lace might've been too much for even the two of them.

"Sunny, I can't help you," her mother said. "You're going to have to work this one out on your own." And she hung up.

Colors

The property management lady looks at the signature on the lease. "We rent mainly to young urban professionals like yourself, but we have some older tenants like me who have been with us for years. You should really enjoy living here." The last is said with a stern stare that says, If you don't enjoy living here, something is seriously wrong with you.

"I'm sure I'll like it just fine." John glances at the keys she holds to his new apartment. He's signed the lease and given her a check, but she makes no move to give him the keys. Instead, she just makes him uncomfortable by staring at his hairline. "Is there anything else?" he asks.

She pulls her gaze from his hair and smiles at his face. "No, nothing at all. You'll fit in fine." She hands him the keys, then rises to shake his hand. "Welcome to the Portland Towers."

He takes her hand. It is soft and dry and frail. "Thank you."

When John leaves to inspect his new apartment, she sits back down and looks over her list of tenants. She's very pleased. Her new tenant is a nice purple, and she's been trying to get more purple auras into Tower Three but so many of them fail the credit check. Greens and reds do fine, but not purple. She wonders what it is about purple auras and bad credit. A building should be a kaleidoscope of auras, and she looks forward to the annual Christmas party where they will all outshine the lights on the twenty-foot tree. It doesn't matter to her that not a single dark-skinned person lives in the Towers. She sees beyond the skin to their true colors.

Upstairs on the fifteenth floor, John lets himself into the apartment and locks the door. He goes to the living room window, sets down his briefcase and takes from it a camera with a long telephoto lens. He steadies it against the frame of the window and looks through it across downtown at the Pearl District. He smiles and would pat himself on his back if he could. There is a clear line of sight to his fiancée's apartment and he can see right into her living room bay windows.

That evening John has dinner with his fiancée, Cindy, downtown at El Gaucho to celebrate his new apartment. Afterward when they walk out together, holding hands, she asks, "Are you sure you don't want help packing?" Her breath makes a cloud in the cold air.

He shakes his head. "I wouldn't subject even my enemies to that. No, go on home." He kisses her.

She lets go of his hand. "I'll call you when I go to bed."

"I'll be on my cell. I'm going to take a load of stuff over there tonight."

They kiss again, this time on the lips, and go their separate ways. Cindy is excited about his new apartment. She hasn't seen it yet, but from what he's told her it is bigger than both of theirs and will serve well for them once they're married and looking for a house to buy.

When she gets to her apartment and lets herself in, she looks at it with fresh thoughts. It's small, but nice, sitting on the tenth floor with a big view of downtown. She sits on her couch and gazes out at the city. It's a clear night. She can even see a few stars through the light pollution. She's going to miss her apartment, she thinks, and sighs.

The doorbell rings and her girlfriend lets herself in. "Honey, I'm home," she calls out, then spots Cindy on the couch and hugs her from behind. Nuzzling her neck along the hairline, she smells steak and restaurant food mixed with her perfume. She remembers Cindy said she was going to dinner with people from her office.

"I wish I could've come," she says petulantly, like a spoiled princess.

"You would've been bored. Nothing but office gossip. Besides, they're not ready for you."

The girlfriend steps over the back of the couch and leans against her. She has short cropped hair and dresses like she's on a Little League baseball team. "That's what you always say. It's you who's not ready." She looks up into her face from where she has slid into her lap. "Don't you feel trapped being someone you're not? Stop worrying about what they'll think."

"We're not having this conversation again." She pets her girlfriend's spiky hair. "I'm tired, it's been a long day."

"Not too tired, I hope."

* * *

Looking through his camera lens, John is in shock. Another man he can deal with, but a schoolboy? What if she's pregnant? It might be the boy's. What if he's a minor? He pulls away from the camera's eyepiece and tightly closes his eyes. That would mean possible prison time for Cindy. He's not going to marry an inmate. His thoughts are spiraling. He looks into the camera again. They're still on the couch, but the boy now has Cindy's shirt open and is working his way downward. John clicks away with his camera, but feels dirty and nauseous, so he stops. He sits down on the floor of his empty apartment, experiencing emotions he doesn't want to experience, nor thought he ever would.

* * *

"I have to make a call," Cindy says as she pulls her blouse together. "I'm sorry, I forgot. It has to do with work and I should call before it gets too late."

Her girlfriend gets up from her knees and sits back on the couch. She's seen the patterns before. She likes straight women and knows when "office" means "guy." "You should leave him, you know. It won't work, you and him." She puts her hands on Cindy's cheeks. "You were meant for me." But she has said that to other women and they didn't stay, and even she doesn't feel any truth in the words anymore. It's just another line.

Cindy smiles at her. Is she really that transparent? "I don't know what you're talking about. It's just work."

* * *

John's cell phone rings in his new apartment. He lets it vibrate on the floor next to the camera. He doesn't know what to say to her. There is no way he can live here now with such a view. He can imagine having a telescope and obsessing on who she's with three years from now. He'll invite friends over and offer them a peep of his ex. He shakes his head and pinches the bridge of his nose. Maybe the management lady will tear up the lease since he hasn't actually moved in. He can always tell her what happened and how his fiancée left his heart black and blue.

Tree House

Twinkles lived in the West Hills of Portland on Vista Ridge. It was a nice neighborhood in that the houses were expensive and large. Families could live in them without running into each other for days, which was good because many of the families' members didn't play well together. Divorce rates were high, affairs a given, and out-of-touch children, who expected life to be sprinkled in front of them like rose petals, were rampant. Twinkles lived in a tree house in the backyard of the Johnsons' house. It belonged to their children, but they had grown up and moved south to California. It was a good tree house, built by craftsmen and made to last. It needed some paint and caulk because the Johnsons were now elderly and without grandchildren visiting it was neglected. Twinkles wanted to paint it and protect its flaking wood, but he didn't want to draw attention to himself. Nobody knew he lived there. He was a tree house squatter and he doubted squatter rights would apply to tree houses.

Twinkles liked squatting. It seemed more natural than ownership. You can't take your house with you, so ownership was really no more than squatting. But people's laws said otherwise and men with guns enforced them, so Twinkles kept quiet in his tree house and only fixed things that wouldn't be noticed, like leaks in the roof and squeaky hinges, and these he did in the early hours of the morning when no one was about except for the drunks arriving home after last call. To them he would appear as nothing more than an apparition of an oversized gnome. He even wore a red hat he'd found last Christmas. It was knitted wool, and it may not have kept his head dry, but it did keep his thoughts warm, and it was important to keep his thoughts warm because it was his thoughts that controlled where he traveled at night in his dreams.

He called them dreams, but they were more than that. They were out-of-body experiences, but calling them that would sound crazy, and he didn't want to sound crazy to the people who worked at the soup kitchen where he got his main meal of the day. It was well known that if one of the do-gooders there thought you were crazy they would fast track you onto heavy meds, and getting that main meal of the day would then become contingent on taking them. Living in a tree house and taking heavy meds was not a good combination for survival.

It was raining hard as he zipped himself in his sleeping bag like a mummy wrapped for centuries of sleep until the grave robbers would wake him. He lay there listening to the pitter patter of angel toes tap dancing in the rain, thinking grave robbers wouldn't find much to steal. The opossums and crows would have a much better haul, which was only fair since he had shooed them out of the tree house when he moved in, and occasionally still had to. His dreams started as a noise, like the ringing people get in their ears, but more of a vibrating sound like high-voltage power lines in a storm. It would grow louder, as if it would wake the whole neighborhood and the Johnsons would amble outside on their walkers, and then with a sudden snap of elasticity, he would find himself suspended in the air outside the tree house.

Tonight he drifted down the street like a tuft of dog fur caught in a breeze, not choosing where he was going but riding the currents of his thoughts. He had only recently figured out he could influence where he went. It was strange being a living ghost inside a strip club, but very much the same. He still couldn't touch the girls, and he heard them say what he sensed from them anyway. They talked about the men who ogled them on stage, about how they hated dancing for them, but couldn't dance without them. One night he sensed something different from one of the dancers than the usual dislike and disgust and left with her. He sat in the back of her car as she drove. He knew it was a creepy thing to do, but the whole thing was insane to start with so he did it anyway. He waited for her when she stopped for cigarettes, and when she got pulled over for rolling through a stop sign, he saw how old she was on her driver's license. Sixteen. The cop was going to give her a ticket, but ended up hassling her about being out past curfew. She gave him a sob story of lies and he let her go.

She made a lot of money at the club, and was easily the most popular dancer. She worked it for every dollar she could because she knew it wouldn't last. Nothing did. Eventually her pert looks wouldn't be so pert. She went for the punk and Goth outfits because they made her look older, but not too much older. The other girls at the club told her she should do the Catholic Schoolgirl thing; she still had hers from St. Mary's Academy, but she was afraid if she did that the club manager would start to worry that the ID she used to get the job was fake. Obviously it was fake, but a very good fake. Like so many things, she'd gotten it from a guy who knew a guy. She never considered that the manager knew it was fake and just didn't care. She wasn't that cynical, but maybe she should've been.

But Twinkles' thoughts didn't lead him to the strip club at the bottom of the hill tonight, instead he drifted the few blocks to what at one time had been his house and was still where his wife and son lived. She had remarried, but they had never divorced. He'd been declared dead once the requisite time had passed since his disappearance. Since one morning just like every other morning he'd stepped on a bus to go downtown to work and never made it home, at least not in body. Something happened that day inside his head. Like he'd been hoping for all his life, everything became clear, but at the same time, nothing made sense anymore. He didn't hear voices. That would be crazy. He simply "understood". He did talk to himself, especially about his nighttime travels—he couldn't tell anyone about those—and sometimes a voice answered him back, but he knew it was just himself telling him what he needed to hear. "You're a good man, Twinkles. Your travels are your gift. In time you'll know what they are for." It was New Age mumbo jumbo to ease his anxiety when the buzzing started at night. Being loose from his body scared him. What if he couldn't get back and got stuck as a ghost while his body lay there in the mummy bag, unaware that it needed to get to the soup kitchen and eat? He tried not to think about it.

Visiting people in their private moments wasn't the way to endear himself to them, or them to him. Recently he felt he could read their thoughts when he was alone with them. Like the sixteen-year-old stripper when she got pulled over. She was afraid the cop would find out she was a runaway, but the cop was thinking about his own daughter and just wanted this girl to get home. He hated patrolling the night shift. He thought the darkness would hide the ugliness, but it highlighted it instead, like sharp rocks sticking out from the water's surface, waiting for the unsuspecting ship in the night. He sensed her thoughts when she drove away and fantasized about moving to California where it was warm and dry, and now as he drifted through his old house to his teenage son's room, he sensed him dreaming in his sleep of a girl he would soon meet, a punk, sometimes Goth girl who looked older than his own age but really wasn't.

He watched his son breathe. In, out, in, out, and then he heard the buzzing that came before he separated from his body, but it wasn't his buzzing. It was coming from somewhere or someone else.

A voice behind him said quietly, "Dad?"

"I've met a nice girl for you," he said reflexively as if he'd never disappeared on the bus that morning.

"Dad? Is that you?"

He turned and recognized his son's figure floating before him. He was about to tell him the girl's name when he was suddenly back in his tree house, zipped snugly in his mummy bag, rubbing his eyes awake as he realized the drumming on the roof of a rain shower had woken him. This didn't bother him, though. Night would be back soon enough.

The Handout

Al wanted so hard to put his frustration into words but there was so much of it, all that came out was, "I'd rather be lonely, than phony." And then he swung at his son-in-law from across the little round caf⊠ table and knocked him out of the cheap wood chair. Al stood up and threw the table aside to get at him. As his son-in-law tried to rise from all fours, he kicked him in the ribs, and when he curled up to hide in a fetal position he kicked him again in the guts. Like so many in life, one punch and two kicks was all it took to turn this hulk into an infant.

The anger released, now he could speak. "You're a drunk looking for a handout, cash so you can go on being a drunk and making a mess of the lives around you. No more. This tit has run dry."

He became aware of the people around them staring. What do you do when your little girl marries a loser? Al didn't know. He left him lying there on the floor in Starbucks. Choosing losers ran in the family. He'd done it when he married her mother. But he'd rectified that by divorcing her, and she'd gone off and married a complete loser. He shook his head to himself as he walked down the sidewalk. All of it was so tiring, he wondered why he got out of bed in the morning. He could afford to sleep in if he wanted. Christ, he could afford to have someone come in and massage his feet twice a day. That was why he didn't see himself as a loser; he'd made money, but he knew there were other ways of being a loser than hitting up your father-in-law because you thought he'd be a soft touch, being sick and all, and you were just too lazy to go to work or too hung over.

He rubbed the knuckles on the hand he'd hit him with. It would be all purple by nightfall, but nothing felt broken. He was glad of that. The nurses at the clinic had told him to be careful, that his body would have trouble mending if he broke anything now with the cancer in his bones. They drip fed his arm a bag of clear syrup to help make his bones strong. They said it was like filling in the holes in a block of Swiss cheese. He guessed it was working, he thought as he flexed his hand and kept walking.

He should've known something was up when Dean had asked to meet him at Starbucks. Shit, a Starbucks. He hated those places with their hyper employees asking how he was and if he wanted a biscuit like he was a dog and would next have to play dead to earn it. When Al sat down with Dean, he let him do the talking. It was just past noon and the guy already smelled of beer. He talked about his fear of losing his kids, how Tracy, Al's daughter, might leave him. They were behind on their mortgage. He even cried a little when he said he didn't know what to do. He needed money to make it all not happen. Would Al please help him out?

Al considered giving him the money. The crying pushed his buttons. He'd been crying a lot himself recently and knew what it meant for a grown man to cry in front of others, but when Dean said they'd have to keep it a secret from Tracy, Al realized he was being played and was just another in a long line of people this guy used to get what he wanted with as little effort as possible. What were a few tears to him? They were easier to shed than to go to work, pick up a hammer and finish a job. Dean didn't care what the runoff would do to Tracy or their kids. It was all about him and nobody else. That was when Al hit the son of a bitch.

Al pushed on down the sidewalk. So much for getting a ride to the clinic. He was going to be late for chemo, if he could be late for chemo. He'd have to take a cab across town. No, forget that, they could wait. He'd take a bus. He was on his own schedule and couldn't be late for anything.

* * *

Dean rubbed the side of his face where Al had hit him. Damn, the old man could still hit hard. A woman nearby moved to his side and asked if he was okay. He nodded and mumbled that he was fine, now embarrassed at the scene the old man had caused, but not too embarrassed to notice that she was good looking, and his type. He liked the busty maternal ones. But he wasn't just embarrassed, it was more. He'd humiliated himself in front of the old man because he was absolutely convinced he'd cough up the money and his problems would go away. But Al hadn't. He called him out instead. Bastard, he didn't drink any more than those around him. Look at his wife's mom and step-dad. Jesus, they were a pair. A matched set of liquor bottles supporting the family members between them with handouts and lies. At least they paid out when you kissed the shit off their asses.

"Sir, are you all right? Can I help you up?" It was one of the Starbucks employees, an emasculated guy in tight black jeans and multiple body piercings showing above the neck. Dean hated that stuff as much as Al hated Starbucks. He shook his head no and started to get up, and when the guy reached out to help him, Dean knocked his hand away and snapped, "Don't touch me, man."

Dean walked back to his truck. He was pissed, frustrated, and still didn't have the money. Tapping Al had been his last resort. He could go to his own parents, but he knew what they would say. He could go to his wife but he'd gone to her the last time he'd needed a lot of cash. She'd given it to him, had to sell a bond, but it hadn't gone so well between them afterward.

Dean was a contractor. He remodeled kitchens, bathrooms, added on decks, that sort of thing. He was a one man show who took half the money up front and the other half upon completion. Dean's problem was completion. He'd taken a lot of people's money and not finished their jobs, and in some cases had barely started. Now people were after him to finish the jobs or give them back their money, but he'd spent their money long ago and didn't have the cash or the credit left to buy the sinks and counter tops and supplies to finish the jobs, not to mention the humiliation he'd face dealing with these people again after months of blowing them off. No way was he going to go to them, hat in hand, and apologize for leaving them with a gutted bathroom for six months. Besides, some had paid him so far back it would be like working for free, and he didn't work for free. No, he'd have to go to his wife again. She'd sell a bond or whatever she did last time to get the money and pay these people back for him. He'd catch hell from her but he'd still come out ahead. At least when it came to the cash. She'd put him on probation, but that wouldn't last. It never did.

He felt better now, sitting in his truck with a plan he knew really would work. He should never have gone to Al. He should've seen that fist coming. But he'd been so sure Al would come through for him. What if he was wrong about his wife? What if the things he'd told Al were true? What if she left him? He filled with dread as he heard her voice in his head, "No, Dean. Clean up your own mess. I'm tired of changing your diapers. These tits have run dry, too." Anxiety tightened around his chest. She wouldn't do that, would she? No, not with the kids. He'd talk to her tonight after the kids were in bed. She wouldn't be able to shout at him then or she'd wake them and they'd come downstairs crying because Mommy and Daddy were fighting again.

He started the truck and pulled into traffic. He'd go to the pub, have a few beers and think it over some more, figure out how to spin it for his wife. Just the thought of the beer helped already. The tension in his chest eased. Things wouldn't look so bad after the second beer and they just might start looking good. Christ, he might even think of someone he'd overlooked who he could go to first.

* * *

The clear plastic bag of Taxotere hung on a chrome rack next to where Al sat in a row of pale green recliners. It was a green Al wouldn't choose for his home. Few would. It was the color found only in hospitals and chemo lounges like this one. Al thought about the color whenever he sat in the row of chairs that ran the length of the room. He was bored with the thought, but he still had it every time. It was like scratching a fleabite from his cat, he had to do it. But he wasn't supposed to scratch at fleabites, or bites from mosquitoes or spiders because they might get infected. He couldn't even shave with a razor anymore. They had him using an electric, which made his skin itch and left him feeling like he'd never finished his morning ritual, the same ritual he'd gone through every morning ever since he started shaving in his teens. Al wasn't averse to change, as long as it was on his terms, but none of this had been. At least not directly. It's not like he ran a stop sign and wrecked his car. But he would cope. He had in the past.

When he was twenty he got his girlfriend pregnant. It was the Sixties and he was from a middle class family, so he married

Dolly and she bore their first child, followed by two more. But before he married her, his father sat him down and gave him a talk. He was a friendly guy who was good with a joke, but rarely got serious. He didn't preach about Al's obligation to marry the girl and provide a home for the coming baby, that went without saying. Instead he talked about how much of life was random and beyond our control. But we did have control over some of it, and we owed it to ourselves to do our damnedest not to mess that up. Al knew he meant getting Dolly pregnant, but he also knew it applied to other things, too, and he carried those words with him ever since and made them his own. Can I control this? Can I control part of it? Did I do the right thing? What was the right thing?

He sat in the pale green Naugahyde recliner and watched the fluid drip from the bag into the tube that led to the vein in his arm. There was at least an hour of fluid left. He stopped watching it because that just made it drip slower. He had to make a call, but the nurses didn't allow cell phone use in the clinic, so he stood up and took his bag of Taxotere with him to the bathroom. It hung on a metal rack that resembled a coat rack with wheels. He got it into the bathroom behind him, closed the door and sat on the toilet seat to make his call.

* * *

"Hello?"

"Hi, honey. It's your dad."

"Hi. Did Dean get you to the clinic on time?"

"I'm here now, but I took the bus."

"The bus? Why? Dean promised me he'd take you."

"Well, honey, I hit Dean. He made me really mad and I hit him."

"What did he do?"

"He asked me for money, a lot of money."

There was a pause. "How much money?"

"Fifteen thousand. He said he owed a lot of people money. Look, if you guys need money, I can help you out, but Dean wanted to keep it a secret from you, make it seem like it was money he'd earned. So I hit him and told him no and said some other things. I'm sorry, honey, but you married a loser."

Tracy started crying. She felt anger, sadness, and frustration all mixed together like a bad soup made of the leftovers of her marriage. "I'll have to call you back."

"I'm sorry, honey."

She hung up and swore loudly, her voice echoing in the empty house. She'd bailed Dean out before, and the last time she'd made it clear that would be it, no more. And now he needed bailing out again and for the same reasons as before. He was too lazy to finish the jobs he'd already been paid for and would rather waste his time in the pub with his pals. She hadn't married a loser, she'd married a man who wouldn't grow up, someone who still needed his socks turned right side out. She'd fallen in love with his boyish charm, his what-me-worry smile and easy manner, but now it manifested as one excuse after another for not doing what needed to be done and always ended in him saying he was going to take a nap.

She turned off her shows, dabbed her eyes with the back of her hand and went to the kitchen where she poured herself another cup of coffee. Now instead of picking him up, brushing off his knees and wiping away his tears, she would have to be the tough mommy, the disciplinarian, and dammit, that was not what she signed on for. She wanted a partner, not a child who liked to drink more than work.

She carried her coffee into the bathroom and fixed her eye makeup. Tomorrow she would wear the waterproof kind. This was going to be one of those weeks. When she was satisfied you couldn't tell she'd been crying, she went back to the kitchen and called her husband. He better come clean with her. How much did he really owe? She'd have to know that before she'd know whether to play hard ass with him or to hold his hand. Either way, she wasn't selling off any more of her inheritance to pay off the people he owed. She'd done that before and someone else could do it this time. She'd send him to her dad again, but this time with her blessing.

* * *

Dean's phone vibrated on the bar.

"The little woman?" Stay Puff, the bartender, asked as Dean checked the number on the screen. His friends called him Stay Puff because he resembled the Pillsbury Dough-boy.

"Yep," he said as he flipped it open. "Hi, babe."

"Where are you?" she asked coldly.

Her tone told him what had happened. Crap, he hadn't thought of that. "Getting some lunch."

"My dad called. Why are you asking him for money without talking to me first?" Then she lost it. "Whose fucking dad is he, anyway? You asshole."

"Look, I'll come home. I'll explain everything."

"You bet your ass you're coming home. Do you really owe fifteen grand or did you pad it so you can loaf?"

"Babe, I'm leaving right now, okay?" he said and hung up.

Stay Puff could tell from what he overheard and from what he knew of the little lady that his favorite customer was in the shit with the wife, something he was too familiar with. He picked up Dean's pint glass and topped it off, then did the same with his own. "You still want that burger? It's on the house."

Dean sucked the foam off his pint. "I'm in so much trouble."

Stay Puff smiled reassuringly. "Then what's another hour? I'll go see if it's ready."

* * *

In a bar across town from Dean's pub, Ray spooned soup into his mouth at a table not far from where the bartender was propped in front of his lunchtime regulars. The bartender, an anemic man in his forties in need of a shave, was telling a story about one of the Happy Mouthful's patrons from the old days, Jimmy Drake. The four regulars hung on his every word, their eyes flicking back and forth between their frothy pints and the bartender's lightly spittle covered lips. He was one of those people who foamed at the mouth when they talked, especially when animated like he was now.

"Jimmy had been drinking all his life. He started in high school on the weekends, and soon the weekend started on Thursday, then Wednesday. In college nothing changed. He joined a frat and they partied all the time. He graduated, got a good paying job, got married, had kids. He was living the American dream. He was deep in his forties and all was going well when for whatever reason his wife gets on his case about his drinking and wants him to quit. I think she read some article in Newsweek about the perils of alcohol or some such shit. So now the guy can't have a drink at home without the wife nagging at him, and if he makes up for it at the bar, she nags him twice as hard, so he gives in and quits drinking. He starts jogging and going to the gym, he loses a bunch of weight and looks great and guess what? He's dead within the year from a massive heart attack." The message was clear. Drinking kept you alive.

The bartender's gaze landed on one of the regulars who was finishing his pint. "Another one, Bill?"

Bill set the glass down and nodded. Who wouldn't after that story.

"What about you, Howard?"

Howard nodded, too.

Ray chuckled into his soup. He'd heard the story before in other bars in other cities in other countries. Every pub had a Jimmy Drake, and Ray laughed at the truth in the myth, not because he was a drinker and stories like Jimmy's comforted him as the suds went down, but because he'd given it up a couple years back and according to urban myth and stories like the bartender's he should be dead by now. But he could relate to the heart attack. Ray didn't miss the hangovers, the anxiety, depression, or the thirst and fear of what he would feel like if he didn't start drinking soon the next day. He didn't miss any of that. What he missed was the escape. When he got home after a night out and sat drunk in front of the television sipping a beer and smoking a cigarette, nothing bothered him because he'd reached that state of drunken nirvana where he felt nothing, no anxiety, no fear, no unhappiness. This was his holy grail, this was what he spent his afternoon and nights trying to achieve, a state of nothingness free of idiots and pain. Sometimes he made it, sometimes he failed.

Ray went back to his soup. After he'd quit drinking he soon found that idiots and pain were the norm, or at least his norm for that period, and he would have to learn to cope or he might as well go back to drinking again. Be an idiot to escape the idiots, or learn not to be an idiot and not to let the idiots get to him. One glance at the regulars saddled at the bar reminded him of why he'd chosen the latter.

It was chemo Tuesday, and after lunch he drove out to the clinic on the east side of town to pick up his father. When Ray pulled up in front, the first thing his dad said when he got in the car was, "One of the girls in reception wants to get together for lunch."

All the women who worked in reception were a lot younger than his dad, so he asked why, but he knew why. Al drew wounded birds to him like shit does flies. He was smooth and could talk the talk and make you feel hope when you were so blue all you wanted to do was crawl back in bed and sleep.

"She wants to talk," his dad said.

"Which one is she?"

"She's the one I see on my way out who does the scheduling."

Ray knew who he meant from when he used to go with Al to his appointments back in the beginning, and he'd gotten the same vibes off her as he had from Al's last girlfriend. Wounded birds rarely brought much to the table other than their "please fix me, but don't hurt me doing it" stance. But now his dad was going to add a new dimension to it.

"Al, she's my age." Ray pulled into traffic.

"It's just lunch."

They both knew it was more than just lunch, and Ray wondered who his dad was that he favored people he could play father to over those he couldn't. Now they were age appropriate to being fathered. Hopefully it would only be lunch, but Ray knew that was wishful thinking.

Al rubbed his hand and looked out at the passing houses. "I had a fight with Dean this morning."

Ray laughed as he drove. "You've been busy today. What was it about? Were his lips too chapped to kiss your ass?"

"Something like that. He wants money."

"How much?"

"A lot."

"Did you give it to him?"

"No, but I probably will."

Ray had little to do with his sister and brother-in-law, but that hadn't always been so. When he first moved to Portland it was because he wanted to be around more family, actually have a Thanksgiving instead of going for Chinese. He was living in Boston, the same as Al before they diagnosed his cancer, and wanted to get out from under his shadow. But it didn't play out the way Ray had daydreamed it would and anybody with half a brain could have seen that it wouldn't.

When he started visiting his sister's house, he soon found that being the brother-in-law wasn't going to go well. He got along with Tracy and Dean fine, but when the drinking commenced he'd leave because he saw no point in talking to someone with that third beer glint in their eyes. Sometimes when he would visit, the drinking would have already begun and he'd want to leave the moment he got there, but he'd stay long enough to make a polite exit. When that happened several times in a row, he stopped visiting in the evenings and switched to the afternoons, but that was an equal failure. By mid afternoon Dean had already been hitting it at his pub, and Tracy was irritable and short tempered because she was hung over but thought it was too early to start drinking, and they were uncomfortable to be around as they got angry at their kids over nothing, Dean because he was holding back on the beer to keep up appearances, and Tracy because she was tired and feeling the thirst. So Ray stopped visiting altogether. This was back when he'd been sober for less than a year and was still working it out and much more sympathetic to drinkers because he still saw himself as one. But not anymore. Now he had no patience for them. But there was more.

"Buy him a suitcase of Coors. He won't waste a drop of that." Dean pulled to a stop in front of Al's apartment. After more than two years of not drinking, Ray was still angry at himself for wasting so much time with the stuff and he took it out on those making the same mistakes he had. "Give him the money and you might as well be paying for his beer."

* * *

Everybody in the boy's immediate life drank. Mac's mother and father, Dean and Tracy, his grandparents on both sides, his parents' friends. Tracy and Dean thought he was too young to think anything of it, but they were too busy drinking or hung over to be aware of the subtle impact it had on all those around them. Mac was old enough to know though that his grandparents always smelled like wine, and on the rare occasion when they didn't they weren't very friendly. He knew his dad smelled like spilled beer and so did his mother and they would both get mad easily until TV time after dinner where they drank more and smiled more. He was old enough to have figured out that happiness came out of a can or bottle and he wondered why his parents didn't let him drink. Not until you're old enough, they'd say. It was like they were trying to keep happiness all to themselves. But he'd tasted his dad's beer when he wasn't in the room and it had tasted awful. They could keep their beer and wine because he had a secret. Unlike all the adults he knew, he could be happy without it. But he worried that when he got older happiness wouldn't come from inside him any longer and he would have to drink it like his dad, always needing a can nearby or a bottle to be happy.

When Mac snuck a taste of it, his older brother, Alec, had refused to. In school they had told him it was bad for you.

"Then why does Dad drink it?" Mac asked Alec.

Alec shook his head. He didn't know. "Maybe it's not bad for him?"

"Maybe it is but he doesn't care. Dad drives fast and Mom says that's bad."

Alec shook his head some more. "But Mom drinks, too."

Mac and his brother solved nothing, but they became fairly certain that even though adults spent a lot of time telling others not to do them and knew they were bad, they did them anyway. And if their mom and dad did this, it meant it was okay and that they could do it, too. They could tell someone not to do something and then go do it themselves. But that wouldn't include the drinking for Mac because that stuff just plain tasted bad.

He was watching TV, but not really watching it. He'd seen it before and he was kind of bored. Alec sat next to him on the floor eating his ice cream and rattling his spoon against the bowl. Their mom sat behind them on the couch.

"Stop it with the spoon, Alec," she said.

Alec turned and looked back at her. "What? I'm just eating my ice cream."

"You know what I mean."

Mac hit his brother on the shoulder and pointed at his eyes. She'd been crying and she'd only get angry if he asked her why. He'd asked her where Dad was and she'd answered, work. She'd said it angrily like work was a bad thing. Maybe it was. He didn't like homework. It was definitely bad. Maybe all things he didn't like were bad. He'd ask Mom about it sometime when she hadn't been crying, maybe later tonight after dinner when she was full of bottled happiness.

* * *

When Dean got home he brought a pizza from the pub as a peace offering for being late. Without a word Tracy took it form him and carried it into the kitchen. She was nauseous with emotion and couldn't eat, but the boys always could.

"Hi, Dad," they said in unison from in front of the television.

"Hi, boys." He followed Tracy. "Sorry I'm late, honey. Something came up."

She took one look at him and knew nothing had come up. His eyes were bloodshot, his movements were exaggerated and he reeked of beer. All that had come up were more pints at the pub. She knew his rationale, had even hoped against it. He was already in trouble so what difference did a few hours make, like she was his mommy and to be avoided because she administered the punishment. But Dean had begun to see her as part of the problem because she got all bent out of shape about what she called adolescent behavior and said things like he wouldn't step up. None of that stuff was important, not after being at the pub all afternoon.

Tracy put the pizza in the oven. "Later, Dean. We'll talk about it after the boys are in bed."

"I'm really sorry, babe."

She turned on the oven and then turned on him. "No, you're not. You're not sorry one damn bit." She glared at him, wanting to say more, to shout, to scream, but she held it all in, not trusting herself in front of her boys.

He stood there and shuffled awkwardly on his feet. He pawed at her shoulder but she pushed him away. Her eyes welled with tears, she went back to the living room, and Dean went out to his shop in the garage. When he came back inside a little while later he was carrying a can of beer.

Tracy looked at him from her perch on the couch. "You're unbelievable." But then she thought, the hell with it, and gave in. She went to the kitchen, got herself a beer and returned to the couch. She sat in silence behind her boys, the only sound coming from her were the sound of her sips.

* * *

That night as Mac and Alec lay in their beds up in their room, listening to the muffled argument downstairs, Mac thought about how the bottled happiness hadn't worked tonight. He wondered why it hadn't, and if it didn't work why did they drink it? Even if he was really thirsty he couldn't drink that much water.

The Brother

The length of ticker tape dangled from the boy's small hand, the symbols printed on it resembling cuneiform. Fitzpatrick McClellen was six years old. The tape was from a parade in San Francisco celebrating the return of the troops at the end of WWII. His father, John McClellen, had brought it back for him. "What is it?" Fitzpatrick asked.

"It rained from the sky, reams and reams of it," his father said.

"What do I do with it?"

"Keep it in a place where it'll be safe. It'll make you laugh when you get to be my age," his father said, squeezing the back of the boy's neck and smiling at his wife, Ellen.

He knew his son only from the snapshots and letters Ellen sent him when he was in the war, and they'd been married only seven and a half months before his enlistment after the Japanese bombed Pearl Harbor. To get to know one another again after being gone for so long, John wanted to take his family camping.

"Camping, what's camping?" Fitz asked when his father first mentioned it.

"Well," his father answered, "you go out and find someplace quiet, someplace where nobody else is around, and you live there for a while."

And that's what I'm doing now, Fitz thought to himself as he watched the ants on the sandy ground of the Sedona Canyon, living in a quiet place. Seated Indian style in his khaki shorts, he leaned forward to study the ants closer. Ants on their way out of the campsite were carrying crumbs of cornbread from a muffin that had fallen under the camp table during dinner last night, while others carrying nothing headed back for more.

Fitz picked his nose. He wanted to know if the ants would carry just anything. He rubbed the booger off his finger into their path. An ant inspected it, and then went around it. The next one did the same. Fitz's respect for ants began to grow. Standing up, he wanted to know where they were taking the yellow crumbs. He wanted to know where they lived. He wanted to know if they lived in a quiet place. Hunched over with his hands on his knees, he followed the ants' path out of the campsite. His mother called after him, telling him not to go far, the stew would be ready soon. His father watched, smiling at his own memories of being a young boy tracking ants. Where did they go? And always with such purpose.

For roughly forty yards, Fitz followed the ants through the tumbleweed and cacti to a patch of hard-packed earth with a hole in it where some went in and others came out. He crouched down on his hands and knees, put his ear close to the opening and listened. At first he heard nothing. It was quieter than the campsite his dad had picked. No sounds from the fire. No sounds from people. He lifted his head and smiled at the ants going in and out of the hole. This was a very good place, he thought, very quiet. His esteem for ants grew more. But then a quiet buzz sounded near him, very near him. It sounded like a cricket, but it grew louder. He stood, turning toward the threatening rattle.

At the sight of the coiled rattlesnake, a soothing calm washed over Fitz. He'd never seen a real snake, but now as he returned the snake's stare and listened to the rattle buzz, he felt as if he'd seen this snake before. Not in a magazine, nor in a movie, but somewhere else, somewhere real, somewhere even more real than this.

Leaning closer, he smiled at the snake. "I know you," he said gently. Heavy footfalls rushed through the tumbleweed behind him. "I know you," he said again. The snake rattled its tail, ready to strike. Fitz was unconcerned.

"Fitzpatrick," his father said quickly from behind him. "Stay still, don't move." His army Colt in his hand, he flipped the safety off with his thumb and took aim at the snake. But the trance was broken, the moment lost. The snake struck as the father squeezed the trigger. The gun's report echoed off the canyon walls. On the ground, the snake lay across the ants' trail, its bloodied body severed, lifeless.

"Did he get you?" the father asked, spinning the boy around by his shoulders to face him, but Fitz continued to stare at the broken snake. "Did he get you, boy?" the father asked again. "Look at me, son."

Slowly, Fitz turned his head and looked at his father. "Dad, it wasn't his time," he said, his voice sad.

At the sight of two red dots on his son's thigh, the father's voice carried despair into the depths of the canyon. He crouched down, lifted Fitz's leg and sucked on the bite, spat, then sucked again. He then picked the boy up and carried him back to the campsite.

"What's happening?" the mother asked.

"Snakebite."

"My god."

"Put the fire out," the father said, carrying Fitz to the Ford. "We need to get him to the hospital in Sedona." He put him in the truck, then went around to the driver's side, got in, and started the engine. Ellen piled dirt on the fire, then joined them in the Ford. With a plume of dust trailing them, they made their way up the single-track road to the main highway. The rear tires gripped the old asphalt as the father turned toward Sedona, thirty-five miles away.

"I don't feel good," Fitz said. "I don't like this."

His mother hugged him to her, saying, "Hang in there, Fitz baby, hang in there."

The hospital in Sedona wasn't much. More of a clinic, really. When they rushed Fitz in, he was unconscious. A young nurse and a doctor put him on a gurney and wheeled him into the room that served as the emergency room.

"What happened to him?" the doctor asked from behind his spectacles.

"A rattlesnake bit him," his father said.

Holding Fitz's hand, his mother asked, "Will he be all right?"

"How long ago?" the doctor asked.

"About forty minutes," the father answered.

"I'll do what I can," the doctor said. "You can wait outside."

"We don't need to," the mother said, squeezing her son's hand tighter.

"Yes you do, it's policy."

"Come Ellen, let's wait outside. He'll be okay," the father said, taking her by the shoulder and leading her out of the room.

After the door swung shut, the doctor said, "Shit, rattlesnake venom in a forty pound boy. We'll need twenty cc of the antitoxin." He checked Fitz's eyes. There was no response. "He's gone into shock, get that antitoxin."

"Right here, sir," the nurse said, handing him a syringe. The doctor took it, found a vein in the boy's arm and injected it. He felt Fitz's pulse, it continued to grow weaker.

"What can we do for him?" the nurse asked.

The doctor continued to feel his pulse. "That's it, we've done what we can," he said.

The pulse grew fainter. A gentle sigh passed over Fitz's lips and the pulse was gone. The doctor let go of the arm. No pulse, no breath, no life. "Why here?" he said, then turned toward the nurse. "Well, best you go tell the parents."

"But doctor, don't you think that's more your respo—"

"Go on, you got to get broken in sometime," the doctor snapped.

The nurse stared at him, looking at his perfectionist eyes, then looked down at the linoleum floor and walked out of the room. The doctor smiled.

John and Ellen rose at the sight of the nurse approaching them down the hall. She was in her early twenties, but death was not new to her. She had lost school friends who served in the war. Even so, she still felt the bile of anxiety in the back of her throat.

"How is he?" the mother asked. But the father recognized the signs, the hesitant walk, the averted eyes, things the war taught him.

The nurse stopped several paces from them, as if afraid. "I'm sorry, he didn't make it," she said, and then added, "The doctor did everything he could."

"No, this can't happen," the mother said, beginning to rush down the hall, followed by her husband.

In the emergency room, the doctor pulled a sterile sheet over the dead boy, dreading dealing with his parents. It was always the same. It can't happen to me, that only happens to other people. Well, it's time to wake up, the doctor thought to himself, leaning against a stainless steel countertop and looking at the outline of the boy under the sheet. Hell, it could be anybody's boy. Who said god was choosy?

The air conditioner hummed in the window. A corner of the sheet rippled in the refrigerated air. The body's outline was still, but then it moved. The chest rose. The doctor heard the boy inhale a tremendous breath. "This can't be," the doctor said, sliding along the counter away from the body. The boy threw the sheet aside. His eyes were wide, like a startled doe caught in a car's headlights. He looked around the room, amazement and surprise on his face.

The doctor stared. The door opened. John and Ellen rushed in. Fitz exhaled, breaking into a hacking cough. Ellen took him up in her arms. John froze, his face hard, then he looked up, a knot like never before in the back of his throat. He stepped forward and looked at his son, but something was off, something was not right. It was his son in his wife's arms, but the eyes behind the mask had changed. A new player had taken the part of one who has retired.

"Dad," Fitz said.

John looked on, silent, and then smiled. I'm being silly, he thought, "That was close," he said, "you had us scared."

"You shouldn't have killed that snake," Fitz said.

"The snake that bit you?" the mother asked.

A puzzled expression crossed the father's face. "I was trying to —"

"I know, but you shouldn't have," Fitz said. "Can we go now? I'm hungry."

"Sure," his father said.

"I think we should keep him here for a bit," the doctor said, asserting himself as in charge again. "Tests should be done."

The young nurse stepped into the room. Her hand went to her mouth. The mother looked at her and then at the doctor. "You got some yarbles saying that," she said.

The doctor cleared his throat. "Well, he should be observed for—"

"Doc," the father stepped toward him, "shove off." Then, to his son, "Give me a hug, boy." As his son did, he picked him up with one arm and carried him out of there.

After returning to Sedona Canyon, the family packed up their camping gear and started the drive back to their home in Tucson. It was only a few hours, but it had grown dark, and everyone was worn out by the day's events. John tuned in a radio station playing Benny Goodman. Fitz fell asleep between his parents on the Ford's bench seat, Ellen's arm wrapped around his shoulder.

John flipped the sun visor down and pulled a cigarette from the pack held to it by a thick rubber band, lit it with his Zippo and cracked his window. He glanced at Ellen, offering her one. She shook her head no, and he flipped the visor up.

"Why would that nurse do such a thing?" Ellen asked the darkness being pierced by the headlights in front of the truck.

"When she came towards us, I knew what she was going to say. She believed what she told us. That doctor's a witling. The antitoxin just took longer than he expected," John said, then took a drag.

"Something of a miracle, really," Ellen said, looking at her son. "I forget how fragile he is."

John exhaled smoke. "Life's fragile. Sometimes it's just a matter of chance that we make it to the end of the day."

"John, do you want more children?" Ellen asked, her voice quiet, fading in the rumble of the truck.

He looked at her, reading the feelings held in her gaze. "Yes, I would."

"I don't want you to think I'm being morbid but—"

He cut her off, "No need to say it."

They were quiet for a while. John smoked, Ellen looked at the stars on the horizon.

"Do you think Fitz will be all right with it?" she asked.

"Sure," John said and grinned, "As long as you promise him a baby brother."

Ellen was about to say something, but felt Fitz stir. He lifted his head and looked around. His eyes shone in the headlights of a passing car. "Where are we?" he asked.

"We've still got a ways to go," his father said. "How do you feel?"

"Okay," he said, sitting up straight. "I had a dream."

"Tell us about your dream," Ellen said.

"I had a brother, a baby brother at first, but he grew and I grew. His name was Cal, short for Calhoun. He was smart, and liked to laugh. Sometimes he could be mean, but he liked laughing more than being mean."

His parents looked at each other. "You little fibber," Ellen said, poking him gently in the ribs. "You were listening to us talk."

"I think I need a brother," Fitz said.

"And how's that?" John asked, rubbing his cigarette out in the truck's ashtray.

"Everyone needs a brother; you got one." Fitz said. "Uncle Ray's your brother, isn't he?"

John glanced at Ellen. She rolled her eyes and smiled, saying, "We'll see, Fitz."

"When you have him, Mom, can we call him Cal like in my dream?"

"Well, that's if it's a boy," she said.

"Oh, I know it'll be a boy," Fitz said with the overwhelming confidence a kid can conjure up.

"What do you think, John?" Ellen asked, humor on her lips.

"Sure, it's all right with me," he said with a grin, "as long as he likes laughing more than being mean."

"Being mean isn't bad all the time," Fitz said. "Sometimes you have to be. Like you in the war."

"Yeah, like the war," John said.

"Other times you think you have to be mean when you don't," Fitz said.

"Don't tell me, like me shooting the snake," John said with a slight smirk.

"Yeah, like that," Fitz said, then leaned back and closed his eyes.

Ellen looked at John and raised her eyebrows. John shrugged his shoulders, not giving much thought to the words his son was saying, just happy he was there saying them.

* * *

On a dry, sunny day the next summer, Ellen gave birth to a baby boy. The following day, Fitz rode with his dad to the hospital. A nurse, not unlike the one in Tucson, wheeled Ellen to the hospital entrance, where her husband helped her up and walked her to the truck. Fitz was leaning out the truck window, staring intently at the bundle in his mother's arms. When she got in the truck, he didn't touch the baby, but leaned over and sniffed it. Then pulled back and smiled at his mom. His parents paid no attention to his odd behavior. They'd become used to it over the past year.

"Fitz, I want you to meet your baby brother," Ellen said.

"Cal?"

"That's right, Fitz," his father said from the other side as he got behind the wheel.

Fitz held out his arms. "Can I?"

"Of course," Ellen said, giving him his baby brother and showing him how to hold him.

"Get used to that," his father said, starting the truck. "You're going to help raise him, you know."

Fitz looked at his dad, then the baby, then his dad again. "It's hard to believe he'll be as big as you some day."

"And you will too," Ellen said, taking the baby back into her arms.

"When he can sleep through the night without waking, he'll share your room," his father said.

"Like when my friends do?"

"Every night a slumber party," John said. "What have we gotten ourselves into, Ellen?"

Fitz smiled, "I'll tell him bedtime stories."

"He'll like that," Ellen said.

* * *

On the day of the first snow in the Dragoon Mountains, John poked his head into his son's room. Fitz was sitting on his bed reading a thick, hardbound book.

"Whatcha reading?" his dad asked.

"D through F of the encyclopedia."

"And you understand it?"

"Some, the pictures help."

"You like it?"

"Yeah, it's all about another world."

"I guess it would be, compared to a bedroom in Tucson," John said. "Come, give me a hand. It's time we moved your brother's crib into your room."

"It is?" Fitz said, his eyes wide. He jumped off the bed and followed his dad into his parents' room.

John began to roll the crib out of the room. "Make sure I don't bump the walls going through the doorway," he said.

"Got it, keep coming, keep coming," Fitz said, guiding his dad and the crib like he were a signal man waiving his lighted wands at the airport.

That night, after his parents looked in on them one last time before going to bed themselves, Fitz slipped out of bed and climbed into the crib. The movement woke the baby, but he didn't cry, just stared at his brother. Fitz sat down Indian style and returned the stare.

"It's time for me to tell you a story. It's a long one and will take years to tell. I think it's true, at least it feels true," Fitz said, cocking his head and scratching his ear. "And I think I've been sent here to tell it to you, I'm not sure. The story is about people a long time ago, before people were people, back when they were covered with hair like dogs, and the others who came here from far away who had no hair."

The One

Sandra smiled at Jason across the café table, looking at him, but also looking through him. "We can go for walks in the countryside, dance among the wild flowers, and make love in the tall grass." She was as high as she'd ever been on being in love. They'd met three weeks ago, at the end of September, and had been together every night since. It was the start of a glorious fall.

Jason took a bite of his sandwich and chewed. Now that fall was here, he was glad summer was over. He could finally breathe. Sandra would never have liked him when he was knocked out on Benadryl and blowing his nose every other kiss. "I'm allergic to grass. I wouldn't be much of a turn on making love in the grass, unless hives get you going." He leaned across the small metal table and gave her a sloppy smooch, equally high on being in love with the woman he was certain had to be the one.

"We'll find a big rock, as big as a car, and make love on it instead," Sandra said, reaching across and wiping her lipstick from his mouth.

"Someone will have to be on the bottom. That's gotta hurt." He lacked imagination sometimes. That was what they said at work, but he got by.

Sandra leered at him. "No, we'll do it standing up."

His expression was blank.

"Don't worry, I'll show you."

"I'm sure you will." She had shown him a lot. Just when he was beginning to feel middle-aged, he was a teenager all over again.

Sandra glanced at her watch, a big bulky thing with rhinestones. "Oh no, I'm late. I have to get back to the salon or Diane is going to scream at me again about respecting the clients. It's always the clients, they want this, they want that. A bunch of old ladies trying to hide their age by being frosted flakes."

Jason had a lot of gray, but he claimed to wear it proudly even though he would've dyed it if he didn't think it looked as fake as a Hollywood actor with boot polish in his hair. So he wore it short instead, thinking it didn't show the gray so much.

Sandra was a hair stylist in the Pearl, a swanky high rise district downtown that didn't fit in with the rest of Portland's rundown neighborhoods lost in the 70's. Losing your gray was all the rage for people returning to wearing clothing styles very similar to the bellbottoms and wide leg jeans they grew up in. That was the cyclical nature of fashion, doomed to repeat itself, but Sandra wasn't concerned. She rode every trend that hit the streets, from pink iPods to deep brown toenail polish that screamed you had emotional depth. A new fad was an excuse for change, and change was what kept her interested in her surroundings. She got bored quickly, and she knew this was partially why she had trouble staying in a relationship for more than a few months. She had tried, but it always went stale for her, like French bread left out overnight to dry out for turkey stuffing. The moisture of love would evaporate and she'd be left with the unenviable task of letting the guy down softly.

"It's not you, it's me," she'd say. "I have trouble committing. You'd be so much better off with someone like..." And here she would name a mutual friend who was horny and lonely and looking to snare a new boyfriend by getting them in bed. She'd done this a bunch of times, but it still surprised her how easy it was to transfer her ex-boyfriends' affections to someone else if she just got their peckers pointed in the right direction. They couldn't complain about being dumped if they were getting laid within the week. Maybe it was this transitory nature of their love that kept her from ever giving them her all.

She'd been with Jason only three weeks, and the bread didn't usually go stale until sometime in the second month, so she still had a few weeks to enjoy being high, to feel the buzz that being in love gave her. She hoped Jason was "the one," but when she was honest with herself, which she expected she would be soon enough when the buzz began to wane, she would admit to herself that once again she was with the wrong man. Jason wasn't for her. He had allergies, was unimaginative in bed, and his nose was big and not cute like she'd thought in the beginning when they'd first met walking in the Rose Gardens, each alone, physically, and in their thoughts. And he farted in bed. She drew the line there. She never wanted to get that comfortable with someone. Trends were about image and illusion, and a certain amount of mystery had to be maintained for the whole system to work. Without mystery, pointy shoes would just be pointy shoes, and sexy aftershave would simply be menthol stink. Farting in bed brought it all down into a pile of boring routine.

For the first time the other night, Jason had farted in bed. He'd been asleep, or at least feigning sleep, but that didn't matter, and she suddenly realized that where there was a first time there would soon be a second time until it become commonplace. This was why you could never trust a person again after they cheated on you. You would always be looking around wondering who their next lover would be. The cute blond in the perky pushup bra? Or the chubby brunette with the low cut top?

Sandra looked across at Jason as she gathered up her bag and was stricken with withdrawals. Her love buzz had dropped out from underneath her. She'd killed it with her thoughts about being honest with herself and now she was craving prime rib but all she had in front of her was Jason's big nose. She kissed him goodbye and rushed back to work, practicing in her head the conversation she would have with him tonight and deciding who she would point his penis at. "It's not you, it's me," she mouthed. Or maybe she'd wait till morning after she'd given him a parting fuck.

What Are You Looking At?

I was living in the perfect city. The two-leggers who called it home with their "I heart Oregon" and "Diver Down" bumper stickers were a bunch of crumb-dropping couch hogs who couldn't catch me even if they doubled up the batteries in their electric scooters. When it was mealtime I'd head to the nearest supermarket parking lot and pick myself out a nice fat shopper who looked the sort to barbeque year round. They were easy to smell with the scent of animal fat glistening from their pores and they left a stink trail even a puppy could follow in a downpour. I'd watch them go in and then wait for them to come out carrying my dinner. On their way back to their car, I'd tear into the plastic bags and spill their contents across the parking lot, then grab whatever meat they'd planned on grilling that evening.

It was easy pickings. I'd score chicken twenty packs and gorge on drumsticks and thighs, family steak packs that would make me sleep for a day. In summertime I would score sausages galore. In fact I was getting fat just like the tubby two-leggers who were supplying me the goods. I was smart about it. I never hit the same store twice in a row or at the same time of day. I was unpredictable and spread my scores amongst ten or more big chain stores so they never knew when I'd hit them, but eventually enough of the poor sport customers complained and most of the stores hired security guards to keep an eye on things in the parking lot. Calling them security was being kind. They wore their ill-fitting uniforms down low on their hips like gangbangers imitating prison inmates, sported tattoos above the collar and had stretchers in their ears. The acne on their faces said they were straight out of high school or the GED equivalent and dog did they love to talk on their cell phones. They'd sit in their third-hand cars in the remotest part of the parking lot, smoking cigarettes or getting high, and gab and gab on their phones.

"Whatcha doin', bro?"

"Sittin' in my car at work, 'bout to burn one."

"Way cool, dude."

Can you imagine if us dogs used cell phones, had little bluetooths jammed in our ears? The conversations wouldn't be long. It's hard to talk and sniff the hydrant at the same time, and beside, the hydrant can tell me a lot more than any conversation could. But then again there are some neurotic types who, like you two-leggers, would give you a step-by-step accounting of the minutia in their lives because they'd be afraid to hang up and break the illusion that they were not alone.

Two dogs at the dog park doing the usual ass sniffing in greeting when one of their cells rings.

"Hold that ass right there, I gotta take this."

Not much different than two kids doing homework. While in the middle of power hitting the bong, one of their cell phones rings. "Oops, it's my dad, better take this."

If we misplaced them we wouldn't have much difficulty sniffing them out, but they're anathema to who we are. You two-leggers like to do a lot of things at once and give it an important sounding name like multitasking to cover the fact that you're just doing a lot of things crappily, but us dogs don't multitask. When I pee on a tree, that's what I'm doing. I'm not shitting on the toilet, eating a Baby Ruth and smoking a light while talking to my girlfriend on my cell about the new pink sneakers she just bought at Target.

When it was clear the security guys' efforts were inept because, let's face it, it's hard to give chase with your pants sliding down your ass, it somehow became big news on the local television station. I was enjoying the stupidity of a Friskies commercial on a TV in a department store window when Mr. Happy News Anchor came on with a human interest story about how the city was becoming overrun with starving feral dogs who attacked people in supermarket lots for their Twinkies. I guess my efforts to spread my work around had been a bigger success than I realized because this town had the fewest free dogs of any I'd been in. Rarely did I see a dog that wasn't chained to a two hundred-pound-plus ball of blubber, and no one was starving. They were pampered and fat like the two-leggers they were tethered to. Like I said, even I was getting fat in this town and I was doing all the thieving and running. And Twinkies.... Let's just say I ate one once and that was all it took. Never again.

Then Mr. Happy gave a guilt trip about people abandoning their pets on account of the economy. Oh dog, what evil people they were to set free pets who might now have to fend for themselves. Too bad it wasn't true because it would be good for them to rediscover what it meant to be a dog. They'd given up their natural state of running free and sniffing and pissing on everything, and for what? A bowl of the same dry kibble day after day. The monotony of it was mind numbing. The day the first dog started scrounging at the garbage pits of primitive man was the day we put our nose up at our true destiny. Two-leggers should be eating the kibble, not us. In fact, sometimes I think we should be eating the two-leggers, though I doubt all that fat would be good for us.

It was only a matter of time before the inevitable happened. The politicians saw an angle for cheap votes and got involved, making life miserable for everyone with their quick fix schemes, including myself. They hired more dog catchers, and they weren't as stupid as my security guard multitaskers, and since the city wasn't actually overrun with crazed feral dogs, they were really only after me. The odds were stacked against me and it wasn't long before I found myself behind Safeway in a Mexican standoff with three of the county's finest waving their dog catcher hoops at my head trying to get their nooses around my neck.

"Ten bucks to the first one who gets him?" one of the bastards said.

The other two bastards agreed and doubled their efforts.

I made a break for it but one of the nooses got me and once it tightened up and I began to choke there wasn't any point in fighting and making it worse. Most dogs panic at this point, but not me, I'd been through the system before, an ex-con incarcerated for being free. Once you were caught survival didn't depend on physical force but on mind games. If I wanted to get out alive from where they were taking me, I had to become the sweetest, kindest, easiest-going dog in the pound. I had to be that special dog the visiting two-leggers who were in search of last chance love wanted to share their chili with. So that is what I did.

On my second day of incarceration, a family of wide loads waddled in smelling of last night's meat stew and MSG and I knew they were the ones right away. The stains on Junior's T-shirt were fresh enough to lick and I did just that as I turned on the puppy dog charm. They didn't really have much choice but to bail me out. Even the spinster at the counter processing the papers for my discharge was telling them some malarkey about how sweet it was when the dog chose its new family.

"He's a really smart dog," she said, leading me out from behind the counter on a slip leash. I love slip leashes. "He sure lit up when he saw all of you. Like he knew you were coming."

She got that right.

We left the building and started walking toward a full-size van in the parking lot. No minivan for these folks. Junior was a little fatty about ten or twelve and it looked like I was to be his dog. He started calling me Sparky, like that's any name for a dog, and tugging on that slip leash. Slip leashes only work as long as you pull on them. If you slacken the leash and shake real hard, they'll loosen up enough for you to back out of them, and that was what I did. I stopped walking and the leash went slack and I started to shake it loose but before I could slip free, Junior tightened up on it. If I didn't get free now it would only become harder once they got me to their home and into a new form of prison lockdown. There's be fences and doors and probably a choke collar. I had no choice but to bite the kid. I went for his shin and clipped it just hard enough to start the kid's waterworks so he'd drop the leash. He did and I darted out of reach. Mom and Dad stared at me in shock, too stunned to react.

"What are you looking at? I ain't gonna live in your gilded cage binging on chili and ice cream until I'm so fat my hips give out on me and then you euthanize me because I've become too much of a bother. No, fuck that. That's not who I am. My name is Dirt Mouth, not Sparky, and I'll do whatever whenever I want."

They all stood there slack jawed wondering if they'd really heard what they'd heard and I took off running. This town had become too hot. I'd ruined a perfectly good setup by being too clever. So as I migrated north I contemplated the art of begging as apposed to stealing and wondered if I had it in me to beg for food out front of Safeway. I didn't wonder about it for too long; the quick heist was in my blood.

Neurotics

Jim used to smoke cigarettes but not anymore. He used to drink but that went the way of the cigarettes. He used to have a lot of friends, or maybe they were only acquaintances. He wasn't sure if they'd been one and then the other or if friends could even slip back to being acquaintances again. Somehow saying they used to be friends but were now only acquaintances didn't ring true. When they weren't friends anymore they really weren't anything. Either way they had slipped away. Jim did little that was exciting and from the outside he seemed to live a pretty humdrum existence. But inside his head it was different. Like bees in a hive rattled by a kid with a stick, his thoughts never settled. It was numbing how often he thought the same thoughts and he was always on the lookout for new thoughts he hadn't thought before.

They were mainly about people because that was what he was confronted with. If he'd lived on a deserted island he probably would've spent his time thinking about the effects of tides on beach sand accumulation. He thought about people so much that he'd given his informal study a name: Neurotics. What most people perceived as normal behavior in others, he interpreted as a string of micro actions that circled a person's core neurosis. So something like going to the store for groceries wasn't just going to the store because you needed to eat to stay alive, it was going to the store to buy crap food because you needed to stay fat and reinforce your neurosis of keeping your self-esteem in the toilet.

Jim had a friend, or maybe she'd returned to being an acquaintance, who had a dog that got sick with cancer and died. It was painful and drawn out and inspired her to open a pet store where only food containing healthy ingredients was sold. No dog chow loaded with nitrates or red dye number six was allowed. But while she was busy selling food so dogs and cats would stay healthy, she would eat all sorts of junk she knew was bad for her. Oreo cookie double tall frappuccinos, cheeseburgers a dog couldn't keep down—you name it, she ate it. Overweight and without exercise, she'd stew in her own morass of chocolate pudding delight and tapioca dreams and be left staring at the ceiling unable to sleep at 3 a.m. Eventually she'd drift off only to wake late, crashed from her sugar high and feeling depressed about being unproductive.

She'd come to an impasse in her life. She thought her growing disappointment in life was because of her job. She just wasn't that excited about selling healthy food to dog and cat owners. She loved the animals, but some of the owners drove her nuts with their control freak natures, treating their pets like they were their spoiled grandchildren. Jim no longer saw her as a person, but as a jumble of neuroses. She'd rather wallow in her complaints than effect change in her life. That would take effort and she was emotionally lazy and fearful, but mostly lazy.

Her solution to her crossroads was simple. She found herself a guy and made his problems hers. She became so busy with his issues that she no longer had time for her own. It was such a relief to deal with someone else's issues instead of her own, so safe and distant. To solidify her newfound sense of safety, she linked her issues with his, thus dealing with her own became contingent on her boyfriend successfully resolving his. It was the "I'll do it when they do it" pairing. And of course she'd found herself a boyfriend where the likelihood of this happening was inverse to how much he appealed to her. The phrase "It'll be a cold day in hell" came to mind. And just in case he got brave, grew a set, and started down the road of personal growth, she could always distract him in another direction.

Jim saw this pattern in people all around him, this neurosis of preferring to stew in the status quo, even though they claimed to dislike it, than to grow beyond their self-imposed limitations. Sometimes he would catch himself doing it and have a laugh at himself for being a hypocrite. He couldn't toss the first stone in public but in the cacophony inside his head he used a wrist rocket for lots of rocks. This had become his neurosis. He blamed his discontent and loneliness on the inadequacies of others. His inability to accept people for who they were, self-defeating foibles and all, was what forced him into an odd state of self-imposed exile amongst a city of two million people.

As the people he used to call friends once again became acquaintances he spent his time alone in his yard and his interest in his study of Neurotics began to fade. He became more fascinated with his garden and how to create a healthy growing environment for his plants than in understanding people. His plants grew taller and greener as his life became smaller and more stunted. His backyard became his desert island and the tides the mowing patterns of his lawn. First mow around the edge twice, then lengthwise in line with the house, always in the same direction.

General Chang's Chicken

Charlotte was turning over in the tanning bed like a chicken breast skewered on a rotisserie when she had an epiphany. She could've sworn it was her higher self telling her she'd been an evil dog owner in a past life and the streak of difficult dog training clients she'd had recently was her way of making amends. She was so glad it was Sunday and she had the day off, or so she thought. When the tanning bed snapped off, she wiped the sweat off her legs and back, put on her underwear and slipped into her cutoffs. She pulled on her tank top, fluffed her blond bob cut and stepped into her sandals. On her way out she checked her phone for missed calls and messages. She could never hear the ring of her phone over the hum of the tanning bed.

She had one message and it was from one of her clients from hell. "Hi, Charlotte, this is Sophie Long, Hank's meal ticket. He's gone and done it again. It's the fourth pair of Pradas this week he's destroyed. He's cost me more in shoes than his furry ass cost me at the breeder. If he wasn't so cute he'd make a great pair of slippers. I'm at my wits' end. Call me."

Sophie Long was between boyfriends and lonely and had gotten herself a dog on impulse. She hadn't done her homework on matching the breed to her lifestyle and where she would've been better off with a small dog, she'd bought herself a chocolate Labrador puppy because it was cute, cuddly and fuzzy, but most importantly because she knew it loved her on sight when she arrived at the breeder's and it ran right over to her and licked her face when she crouched down to pet it. She never made the connection that the puppy's love for her might have something to do with the scent of spicy chicken on her lips and breath from her lunch at General Chang's where she and her girlfriend had gotten the idea of Sophie getting a puppy after their third mimosa.

Charlotte had suppressed a laugh when Sophie had told her this story. She hated the mis-pairing of people with dogs that were totally wrong for each other, but it was part of what kept her in business and biscuits. Charlotte had a theory that people unconsciously chose dogs that wouldn't fit into their lifestyles in order to force change into their lives. Sophie Long had gotten herself a puppy because she was lonely without a man, was frustrated with her recent string of disappointing boyfriends, and thought a dog would keep her company. Charlotte's take on it was that Sophie had gotten herself a breed of dog that needed to go on a lot of walks and she unconsciously knew she needed to spend more time contemplating nature and thinking about her life and less time in department stores trolling for accessories. Otherwise she would've picked herself up a handbag dog that accented the Prada she so loved.

Armed with a venti coffee from the Starbucks next to the tanning salon, Charlotte called Sophie back from her car. She drove a Mini, not a new one, but one of the older, smaller ones that would fit inside a garbage dumpster. It reminded her of a circus car unloading an endless line of clowns. She had a mental sweet tooth for humorous images, another reason she liked dogs so much. They were always doing something silly, like her old dog that used to get his head stuck in yogurt cartons trying to get that last lick at the bottom.

"Thank God you called back. I can't handle this dog. I thought I could, but I can't," Sophie said. "Do you know anybody who wants a dog?"

Without hesitation and without thinking, Charlotte said, "I'll take him." Since her last dog had passed away she hadn't planned on adopting another anytime soon, but sometimes you had to grab the opportunity when it presented itself. She knew this dog and had loved him at first sight.

* * *

Adding a dog to her life was like having a boyfriend move in. She had to start picking up after herself if she didn't want to find her underwear soaked in puppy spit in the middle of the yard for the neighbors to comment on. Though she had to admit one morning that watching the puppy "kill" her pink panties with a vigorous head shake started out her day with a good laugh. When she brought the puppy home and let him loose, he went on a search and destroy mission through her house. She followed him around as he trotted from room to room sniffing whatever he came into contact with. He found the yogurt cartons in the recycle bin right off, then the television remote in the living room. In her bedroom he trudged through her shoes in the closet and came out carrying a slipper she'd forgotten she had.

Back in the kitchen he pulled on the dish towel hanging from the refrigerator door like a tug toy and inadvertently opened the fridge door. In an instant he'd crawled onto the lowest shelf after a plate of leftover barbecue chicken before she grabbed him and carried him outside to the yard. She waited for him to do his business, and when he did she popped a treat in his mouth and praised him for peeing outside instead of in her house. It had been many years since she'd done housetraining 101.

While working with him over the next couple of days it was clear that Sophie had done very little training with him in the two months she'd had him, if any at all. Charlotte started from scratch, beginning with his name, Hank. He showed only vague recognition when she said it and she didn't know if he had good associations with it or bad. Sophie might've only used it to shout at him as she chased him around trying to get her Prada out of his mouth, and Charlotte had bad associations with the name Hank. Her most recent boyfriend had been a Hank and they hadn't parted friends. She was still trying to get back her prized Red Sox baseball cap from the SOB.

For the next few weeks they were together constantly, just like with a new boyfriend. She even had to clean up after him and encourage him to pee in the right places. He had a penchant for carrying things, sticks, socks, whatever he could get in his mouth, and giving them the kill shake, and it reminded her of the pictures she'd seen of grizzly bears catching salmon in their mouths. The name suited him so from then on she called him Grizz, the little sock-killing chocolate bear.

They worked on his dog manners together and soon he was sitting and staying when asked, and instead of jumping up on people when he met them, he'd sit and wait for his treat. Slowly, he was turning from a crazy, out-of-control puppy into a dog with half-decent impulse control that was a pleasure to be around, and it was only a matter of time before they ran into Sophie. It happened at Home Depot, where Charlotte had taken Grizz to get him used to loud, indoor environments. He was intently watching a forklift move a stack of plywood when a voice from his past squealed, "Hank! Oh my God, you've gotten huge."

Charlotte turned to see Sophie coming toward them with a guy in tow. Grizz wagged his tail and sat as Sophie crouched down to pet him. "Gosh, aren't you the little gentleman. He would've been all over me before." She looked up at Charlotte. "Wow, this is amazing." Then to the guy she said, "Can you believe this used to be my dog?"

The guy half grunted. "You should've kept him. I could've trained him for you."

Charlotte was worried Sophie might want him back but she didn't need to be. Sophie rolled her eyes at her boyfriend's comment and stood up. "Hon, why don't you go get the things you need and meet me back here at the cash registers, okay?" Once he was just out of earshot she said, "He couldn't train a dog. He's barely housetrained himself. Since he started staying over I had to buy one of those little bath mats that wrap around the base of the toilet so I don't have to see the dribbles he leaves on the floor. I had to withhold sex to get him to lift the seat. But he forgets if he's under pressure, like if it's during a commercial break when the game is on, and a game is always on. If urinals weren't so ugly I'd have one put in my bathroom next to the bidet."

"He must be handy to have around if you need something fixed," Charlotte motioned at the home improvement store around them.

Sophie smirked. "Char, I don't do those kind of projects. That's why I live in a condo. We're here for something he needs, don't ask me what." She smiled as she saw him coming back. "He cleans up well and goes home when I tell him to."

"Sounds like a much better fit than this little guy here."

Sophie waved her sandal-clad foot in front of Grizz's face. "Look, Hank, see my new sandals? Guess who they're made by."

And Grizz wasn't sitting anymore but tearing the sandal off her foot and killing it with a violent head shake.

“Mmm, yum,” Charlotte said. “It’s sandal for dinner, is it? We haven’t had that in a long time.”

Summer Breeze

The scent of the bitch next door was making me so crazy with desire that I almost wish Ray had cut my nuts off like most of the poor saps I met out there beyond the yard. It was summer, the windows were open, and the bitch was in heat. She was a Chihuahua, not that I even liked Chihuahuas. When they ran a switch flicked in my head and all I could think was "kill the rabbit." But it didn't matter that she was a Chihuahua, the scent was the same. I'd hump that Chihuahua until my legs gave out and I could hump no more if I could get at her, but Ray was watching me like a cat does a bird on the lawn. Every time I started to tunnel under the fence into her yard he'd find me and fill my hole with bricks.

That fence line was pretty much brick from one end to the other. Only a few spots were left to tunnel and I'd have to dig there carefully so as not to waste them. Brick was the worst. I could chew through wood, hell, I could chew through the wall of a house and pretty much did once when Ray left me in the dog room soon after I came to live with him. I was bored and a cat was mewing outside, so I decided to go through the wall. Once I got started, I found the chewing relaxed me and soon I'd forgotten all about getting outside through the wall and was just chewing for the sake of chewing.

Last night I was going to have a go at the fence again while Ray slept, but he shut me in his bedroom with him, and every time I started licking the wall to soften up the plaster he shouted at me to knock it off and go to sleep. What a jerk. I'd like to see him sleep with the scent of sex jammed up his nose. Ray's like a dog, real persistent. If he was more of a flake, I would've hit that Chihuahua by now and been sound asleep. He ended up making me lie on the bed where I couldn't get at the wall and about halfway through the night the neighbors must've shut their windows because the scent faded and I fell asleep. Dog, was I tired.

But by morning the scent was back, carried strong as ever on the summer breeze, and Ray had had it with me. He wasn't one to get mad and lose his cool, instead when he was pissed he just got real quiet and abrupt and blew me off when I sidled up to him for a butt scratch. When he was really irritated, he'd shoo me out of the room and shut the door, but he didn't dare do that now and give me a chance to go through that bedroom wall. Instead we went for a ride in the Jeep with the top down.

Riding in the Jeep was a blast of scent. Rushing through that many smells at once was like snorting Ajax, but in a good way. From the route he was driving we were going to Tori's, Ray's girlfriend. She was nice as two-leggers went—she smelled of almonds and was always there for the neck rubs—but she lived with Peewee, a dog that refused to grow up. Admittedly Peewee was only six months old but there were certain behaviors that were expected of him at that age and he wasn't measuring up. I sure didn't act that way when I was six months old. Part of his problem was that no one was showing him what he needed to do. It surprised me Ray hadn't shown him. It was his job, but he'd just stand there smiling at Tori as she stood there giggling at Peewee. Which left the problem for me to deal with.

When we got to Tori's, Peewee was all over me at the door, freaking piddling all over the place. I was down with that as it was a sign of respect but putting his paw on my back had consequences. I spun around with a growl, grabbed his neck and pinned him to the floor. He really pissed himself then as his body went slack in my grip. I'd put up with a lot from a puppy, but Peewee did this every time I came over. Some dogs learned the lesson the first time out, others, like this lint bag, needed the lesson repeated again and again. I wouldn't say he was stupid, but his excitement made him so.

Tori shrieked like she always did and Ray let out a string of harsh words. So typical of the two-leggers, they stand around abdicating and giggling and leave it to me to sort out their mess, then get mad when I do what needs to be done. Freaking pecker heads. The two-leggers' indecision drove me crazy. One of the reasons I liked Ray was that he wasn't so bad in that department. In fact I thought he purposefully let that crap at the door happen. He knew Peewee was going to be obnoxious and that I was going to put him in his place, but the pecking order was in a gray area. He didn't want to piss off Tori by telling her what to do with Peewee, so he let me do the dirty work. I didn't care. I'm used to it. And when Tori's out of the room he gives me a butt scratch and tells me I did right. I'd call this aggression by proxy, which isn't saying much about their future together. Or Peewee's future with Tori.

I let Peewee go and walked on into the house. Tori started cuddling him like it was the end of the world and then said a few things about me. I didn't get what they were but I understood the tone. "How can such a cool dog be so mean to a little puppy?" or some such drivel. What a stupid thing to say. Claiming I'm mean when they only see the tip of the meanness that surrounds them. Go back to your TV and your soft couch and slide back into your fog of light particles. Look at how cats torture mice and birds and whatever they can get their claws into. Look at how buses run down anything in their way, or the way little two-leggers pull insects apart. I like to go after yellow jackets myself, but I don't tear their wings off before I eat them. I gnash them in my jaws and it's quick. The worst meanness is propagated by the spoiled Johnnies, the future water boarders honing their skills on the family dog. I know. I haven't always lived with Ray. He knows, too. He pulled me out of there. He stole me and saved my life. I was a day away from biting that kid and then Dad would've gotten out his shotgun and put an end to me.

We spent that night at Tori's. They shut Peewee in his crate, the only time anyone other than me set boundaries for him. Peewee didn't know where he was supposed to piss or poop so he did it wherever he was when he got the urge. You can't live like that. You end up sleeping in your own filth. There's a reason I can reach practically every spot on my body with my tongue. It's called hygiene and you can't keep yourself clean if you're waking up from a nap with a turd stuck in your ear. Putting Peewee in the crate forced him to hold it. Sometimes.

Tori had a really comfortable couch. I made sure they never saw me on it so I wouldn't give them any ideas. They loved to give me rules, but not Peewee. No getting on the bed unless asked. No barking inside. No drinking out of the toilet. No eating off the coffee table. So many rules and I followed all of them, but the world wasn't fair. Peewee broke all the rules and scored loads of rewards, in food and strokes. When they were dumb enough to leave a sandwich on the coffee table in the living room, I got out of there as fast as I could so I wouldn't get blamed when Peewee wolfed it down, but then they'd say I looked guilty and blame me anyway when I'd been nowhere near the sandwich. And worse yet, they wouldn't feed me dinner, saying I'd already had it. Meanwhile Peewee was getting fat on my food, the little cat-loving bastard.

As I woke up on that soft, luxurious couch of Tori's, I was thinking about that Chihuahua in heat. She'd given me an idea. I was tired of taking it and taking it. Peewee had had a good run but his life was about to change. No more sandwiches off the coffee table for him. He was going to learn how to do things and how to do them the right way and if anyone was going to get blamed for missing sandwiches it was going to be him. I was going to make Peewee my bitch.

Pizza

Every morning while Dave sat on the toilet to crap he read another verse of the Tao and its interpretation by Dr. Wayne Dyer. He had a friend he'd known since first grade who had become a Buddhist while in prison, and he'd said it was part of what kept him sane while a guest of the state. Dave figured if it could help his friend in a cell it couldn't hurt him out slogging through puddles in Portland. What he'd gotten from it so far, forty-odd craps into it, was that he shouldn't worry about what other people did or thought, nor should he bother with what he thought about them or what they did. He couldn't control them so why stress about it.

At the end of each section interpreting the verses, Dyer had a paragraph or two telling you what to do to apply this latest verse to your life. Dave usually skipped this bit because they all seemed to amount to the same thing: copy down a pithy line about global harmony, stick it some place where you see it every day and ponder it as you picked the lint out of your navel. If he followed Dyer's directions he'd have to get out of bed an hour early just to read all the goddamn sticky notes on his mirror. But

Dave also skipped the last paragraphs because by then it was usually time to wipe. Dave joked about the book and Dyer's sticky-note approach to world peace, but now in his forties, it struck a chord in him and even though he strongly associated it with the process of elimination, he began to practice some of what he'd learned from it.

At his regular Starbucks he'd been trading smiles and exchanging glances with one of the young women who worked there. He might've been just old enough to be her father but his morning toilet Tao told him he had nothing to lose, so as he paid her for his coffee, he said, "You wouldn't by any chance have any daddy issues you wanted to work out?"

She froze. She looked up at him without raising her chin, then smiled politely like she'd learned to do at Starbucks school, but then the false smile twisted and she simply said, "I do," and left it at that as she moved off to service the drive-thru window.

Dave didn't have any daughter issues. He didn't have any daughters. He was forty-four, but in the relationship department he was still thirty-four. Not exactly arrested development, but shyness early on had gotten him off to a slow start. The following day when he paid for his coffee, she told him it was time for her break and they sat together and talked. It turned out she wasn't as young as he thought and he wasn't as old as she thought, and she didn't so much have daddy issues as issues with men. She liked girls, and sometimes wondered if that was because her dad had never shown her any affection.

"They're better kissers," she said.

He was a step behind. "You like girls because of your dad?"

It was a lot to learn about a person in the first ten minutes of the first conversation you've ever had with them. She had decided not to hold back. He'd asked and she was going to answer everything truthfully and fully. It was a new approach for her in dealing with men, or rather a return to an old approach.

She'd stopped doing it early on when she learned how easily boys wigged out at too much honesty and sharing. They say guys are supposed to lie when girls ask how they look in a new dress, but they same goes for girls when it comes to guys and their fragile egos and inability to grasp complex emotions.

"Well, if you put it like that," she said, "my dad doesn't make me kiss girls any more than your mom makes you kiss boys."

"We've just entered a whole new level of yuck."

"It's your age."

"They've done studies that show women on the pill like effeminate guys because their hormones are all out of whack. Are you on the pill?"

"Yes. My girlfriend's pussy might get me pregnant."

They both laughed. He kept forgetting she liked girls.

Spending her breaks together when he bought his coffee became a regular thing, and it was in the third week that she announced that she'd broken it off with her girlfriend. She smiled when he asked why. "Because I want to go back to dick."

"Who's Dick?"

"I thought I might try yours."

And then he understood. "Oh, dick with a little 'd.'"

"Hopefully not too little."

So they went on an actual date that night. He spent time primping and choosing a restaurant and when he went to pick her up to take her to dinner, they never got out of her apartment. She had dick, he had pussy, and then they both had pizza. After the second go around, they took a break from gorging themselves. It was good, but better once they slowed down after working through some of the initial nervousness of being with someone new.

She was stretched out, her head resting on his arm. "You forget how good it is until you have it again."

He was always trying to catch up with her. "Sex?" he asked.

"Dick," she said dryly.

"Oh."

She sighed. "It would be nice if we could live happily ever after."

He smiled, but his nervousness betrayed him. "Does that ever really happen?"

She closed her eyes. "No," she said and sighed. "I'm going to be craving sushi in six months anyway."

Charity

The echoes of his hard soles rang against the marble walls of the mausoleum as Dave Howk walked its length to the end. He stopped in front of one of the thousands of small square doors that stacked up the walls like bricks in a chimney, and in the bracket attached to the door, he placed a small bouquet of wild flowers he'd gathered that morning. She would've liked them. Gathering them was something she would've done. He stared at the flowers, somewhat perplexed by this annual ritual of his, but his look of perplexity slid into a smile as he touched the door with his fingertips and said, "Happy birthday, baby."

Then the smile was gone and his face was stone and he walked out of there faster than he came in, his footfalls louder than before, each a slap against the face of the day.

* * *

The client was Sam Warbler. He met a woman and fell in love with her and like all things he loved he wanted to own her. Ownership gave him the sense of security he needed to plaster over the deep cracks of insecurity that ran through the foundation of his personality, but the best he could do with her was own her pussy. It said as much in legalese in the prenuptial agreement they signed before getting married. If she shared her pussy with anyone other than him he would owe her nothing when he divorced her, and he would. Ownership meant not sharing. There was a long list of addendums defining what constituted sharing. Gynecologists were not sharing but they had to be women, and no lesbians. The list of addenda was multiple pages.

All the legal paperwork may have said Warbler owned his wife's kooch but he still had a problem. He'd found another pussy he wanted to buy and he could only own one at a time. No two-for-one deals in the US, not yet at least. His wife's part of the prenup was that if he divorced her without cause she would take half of his assets, and even with him squirreling away most of his fortune offshore, hidden from the IRS, that would still be too much.

So Warbler talked to his lawyer and his lawyer talked to Howk. He gave him a copy of the prenup, saying, "Catch her breaking anything in this and there's a bonus for you."

"How big of a bonus?" Howk asked. If he were a dog he'd be salivating as if a biscuit was being held in front of his nose.

The lawyer smiled. "You'll be able to name it, and make it high. The client can afford it."

"Can't they all?"

"This one deserves it. You'll know what I mean when you get a bead on the wife."

Howk smiled wryly back at him. Warbler and his lawyer didn't care if she was cheating or not, just that he came back with evidence that would convince a divorce judge that she was. Warbler needed to make room in his bed for the next Mrs. Warbler. Howk folded the prenup, slipped it in his inside jacket pocket and left, hoping she was cheating, hoping she would make him some easy money by sharing her pussy with a lesbian gynecologist, hoping to snatch that biscuit without having to bury what was left of himself that kept him just this side of good.

He followed Charity Warbler, day after day, shadowing her routine, discovering who she was acquainted with, learning who her friends were, solving the puzzle of what kind of woman Warbler would go to so much trouble to possess only to now want to discard. She was pretty enough, most trophy wives were, but there was something else about her that caused the people she interacted with to smile and be warm toward her, and she in kind. This is what Warbler had tried to buy but had settle for fidelity. Howk tailed Mr. And Mrs. Warbler to a restaurant in the Pearl District and sat at the bar watching them; there was no warmth between them, just cold silence that settled over the table like morning frost.

She wasn't cheating and it didn't look like she was headed that way either. From the date on the prenup they'd been married six years and she'd settled into enjoying her life when she was away from him and going through the motions when she was with him, as if she were the two sides of the moon, one warm and bright with friends, the other dark and cold with him. And then one night she rushed out of the house alone and drove downtown, rolling through stop signs in a hurry, where she went inside El Goocho, a popular restaurant. When Howk went in it took him a minute to spot her. He would've figured she was meeting her husband, but she'd hesitated outside before going in, as if she had to make up her mind about something before going forward.

She sat alone behind a menu at an out of the way table with a view of the crowded room. When the husband came in wearing the future Mrs. Warbler on his arm Howk put it together. She looked similar to Charity, but she gave the impression she was actually for sale, too much gloss, too much California in her smile, where-as Charity had something that couldn't be bought or sold, only given away, and she did that with everyone she touched. Warbler must've lost interest in what couldn't be owned.

Howk watched from the bar and waited. The prenup said nothing about the husband cheating, that wasn't its purpose at the time it was written, and eventually Warbler left with his date and Charity paid her tab and moved to the bar. Howk got up and took the stool next to her before the bar sharks moved in. She was upset, shocked by bad news.

He smiled at her, knowing if she was going to cheat tonight would be the night, but that's not why he smiled at her. He felt bad for her and was a sucker for wounded birds. In the weeks he'd been tailing her, he'd half fallen for her. "Can I buy you a drink?"

"It's my birthday," she said sadly.

Howk jerked his chin at the sizable wedding ring on her hand. "Your husband forget?"

"You could say that."

As the bartender came and left with their orders, Howk made up his mind. "He's a real piece of work, that asshole you've got for a husband."

She looked at him, eyebrows raised. "Do you know my husband?"

"An acquaintance of an acquaintance." Howk didn't like Warbler, he didn't like Warbler's lawyer and he didn't like the deal he'd made with them. All of it left him feeling dirtier than he was willing to live with. He took the prenup from his jacket pocket and set it on the bar next to her.

She glanced at him, surprised, then picked it up and unfolded it. She recognized it and he hated to see the shadow that fell over her face. "Your husband's lawyer hired me to find proof that you've broken something in there, and I mean anything."

Coolly, she refolded the papers and set them back on the bar. After their drinks arrived and the bartender moved away, Howk finished his thought. "Or to manufacture evidence that you have. Your husband doesn't care which."

She sipped her drink and paused to think a moment. "And why are you telling me this?"

"He's an asshole, a bigger one than me—" he sipped his drink, put his glass down, "—and I've got a thing about birthdays."

Again she said sadly, "So have I."

They sat in silence for a moment, then he asked, "So what are you going to do now?"

"Maybe I should sleep with you and you could take that list back to my husband with number seven circled in red. You can use my lip liner."

Howk liked her sarcasm. It fit with his job. He wanted to sleep with her, but he wouldn't go back to Warbler with it. He picked the prenup off the bar and as he slipped it back in his jacket pocket he said, "I'm going to let it ride. I'll tail you around town going through the motions until your husband's lawyer starts to complain about my lack of results."

She glanced over at him. "Then what?"

"I'll string him along some more. Your husband has deep pockets. I can get you at least three weeks before they fire me and hire someone else. I know who it'll be and he'll move fast to manufacture something against you and that'll be the end of it, but you can hide a lot of money in three weeks. At least enough to smooth out the ride. What were you before you married him?"

"I worked the reception desk at the Heathman hotel."

"Nice job?"

She nodded. "Maybe they're hiring." She wasn't being sarcastic.

"That's the idea." He pushed his drink away, knowing it was time to leave, but he had to ask. "Why'd you marry him? There must've been more to it than the money?"

She looked into her drink and stirred it with the red-striped cocktail straw. "He loved me once, and he has his moments when he's very charming. He could charm the shell off a turtle if turtles were his thing. And I thought I could love him, and I think I did for a while. He wrapped me up in beautiful clothes and exotic places, but it's all lies. By the third year I stopped kidding myself and realized I'd married him for his money. I stopped making excuses for his behavior and coldness and saw him for who he was. Like you said, an asshole. I've been trying to decide ever since if it's worth it, my happiness, his money. When you're with someone you're not meant to be with it's lonelier than being alone. When you're alone there's always hope that love will come along, that the next guy to sit next to you might be the love of your life, but when you've sold your soul that hope is gone, evaporated under the glare of the holder of your pink slip. In my case, my husband, Mr. Sam Warbler."

He wanted to run the back of his fingers down her cheek, feel the warmth of her hand on his, but he put some money on the bar instead to pay for their drinks and stood. "I'll be seeing you around."

"Literally," she said.

He smiled as he looked her in the eyes, trying to project something of what he felt toward her, and left.

* * *

He watched her for another two weeks, catching eyes and exchanging subtle smiles, before Warbler's lawyer called asking for results.

"So, Dave, where we at with Charity Warbler?"

"She's coming along."

"The client is anxious to get all this behind him."

"I'm sure he is. You might want to remind him that I see as much of him as I do of his wife."

"Yes, you would. You'd think I'd remember that. So what do you want me to tell Warbler?"

"Tell the idiot his wife isn't cheating. He needs to keep his pants on and let me do my job. You might also want to remind your client that parading California bleach blonds through the bars won't help him in divorce court."

"More money than sense."

After Howk hung up he emailed the lawyer his current bill. The following day he received a check by messenger that included a large bonus as an incentive to speed things along.

That afternoon she was in Powell's Books browsing the literature section in the Orange Room when he moved up alongside her and said, "I got that call from your husband's lawyer. I can stall them another week, maybe two."

She looked at him, her eyes smiling sadly into his. She put her hand on his arm and squeezed, then nodded and let go. "Thank you," she said, almost a whisper, and moved away.

As night approached he followed her out to the east side of town where she rented a ground floor room at a Motel 6. He watched her room door from his car parked in the lot, bemused at this turn in her behavior. After an hour or so, her door opened and she looked straight at him, holding two glasses, and beckoned him to join her with a movement of her head.

He knew not to get involved with the mark, but he'd already crossed that line when he spoke to her in the bar at El Goocho. There was a familiarity about her he longed to touch, to run his hands over, and for her to do the same to him. Two lonely people pushing their pain aside to make contact with another even if only for an hour or two, all the while hoping it meant an end to their loneliness.

He got out of his car and walked through the rain to join her.

* * *

He stopped following her after that. The next call he would get from the lawyer would be the kiss off. What's the problem, Howk, you've always come through in the past. You sweet on her? He'd stonewall them with something about the right opportunity not coming up, but the lawyer wouldn't buy it and would can him, and then start passing the word that Howk wasn't one of them anymore. Well, to hell with that. He wanted to see her again and again; a dam inside of him had been breached but he held back, knowing the business with her husband would have to be resolved first.

But that wasn't the call that came. It was a few days later and the clock on Howk's nightstand read 3:36 a.m. when he picked up the phone and grumbled into it.

"Where is she?" It was Warbler's lawyer, Jerry, and he was on edge.

Howk turned on the reading light and sat up in bed, rubbing his face with his free hand. He could hear the overflowing rain gutter splashing in the puddle outside his bedroom window.

"Wake up, Dave. Where is she? Is she with you?"

He pushed his feet out from under the covers and swung them to the floor, putting things together. He hadn't been following her so he didn't know where she was. "No, she's not with me." The lawyer would be recording this call. Divorce lawyer rule number one: The PI is the first under the bus.

"Then where is she? The client's nervous. She didn't come home last night and he wants to know what to do."

"He should be happy. She's giving him what he wants."

"Then why aren't you getting it on disk?"

"No more Warblers, Dan, I'm through," Howk said and hung up. He thought of going back to sleep, but she was missing and his mind began to run with that. The early morning hours tinged him with paranoia and he began to wonder if Warbler and his lawyer had been playing him all along. He made coffee, dressed, and started looking for her. The self-blame kicked in. He should've been following her, protecting her. He knew he wasn't being fair to himself, but he rarely was.

* * *

It didn't hit the papers until a week later. The Oregonian headline read: Local Charity Leader Missing. The info that followed gave the date she was last seen, said the husband was distraught, and the police were staying mum on all of it. It didn't say if they suspected foul play, but they did when they came banging on Howk's door the morning he was reading about it in the paper. The article must have forced their hand.

"David Howk?" one of the two the plain-clothes detectives facing him on his small porch asked.

Still in his robe and slippers, he said, "Yeah."

"You'll need to come with us. We'll wait while you dress."

Howk looked at the two cops doing their job. Rule ⊠1 of divorce lawyers was complete. He'd been thrown under the bus. That was fine with him. It freed him up to say what he needed to say. "The missing Warbler woman?"

"Yeah."

"You'll want to see my reports."

Once inside the station he told them what he knew from the initial interview with Warbler's lawyer to the day he stopped following her. He told them of the future wife Warbler had paraded around and of the set-up job they wanted for the missing Mrs. Warbler so she'd get nothing in the settlement. He left out the Motel 6.

"I washed my hands of it. She deserved better." He could tell the cops liked him for the dirty side of it. Warbler goes to his lawyer as a go-between, the lawyer hires Howk and Mrs. Warbler goes missing. But then the police scratched a little deeper into Howk's life and learned of the home invasion a few years back that changed everything and didn't like him for it anymore. He no longer fit their profile so they let him go and started looking elsewhere.

Over the next few weeks the cops turned up nothing. She'd disappeared and the case was put aside waiting for a break in it. A string of transit robberies on the MAX line took over the headlines and she was forgotten. That would be the end of it. Gang violence in Gresham would take precedence over a missing socialite. It sold more newspapers. Howk didn't expect much from the cops. He had his own ideas, fueled by unresolved rage from when his own wife had been taken from him. They'd never caught the ones who'd broken into his house, and he'd never had someone to focus his rage on, but this time he did.

* * *

Sam Warbler was rarely alone. At his office there were the employees, at his home, the servants. At the Multnomah Athletic Club he had his handball buddies, and at night the future Mrs. Warbler kept his fear of the dark at bay. She'd been there every night Howk had kept watch, a brand new Lexus in the drive registered under her name. And the missing Mrs. Warbler's Audi had yet to be cleared out of the garage. He'd checked on both. The only time Warbler was alone was during the drive after work to the MAC club.

In a light drizzle downtown, Howk saw Warbler's big Mercedes pull out of his office building's parking garage and fell in behind him. At the first set of lights he pulled up alongside the driver's side and rolled down his passenger window and motioned to Warbler to do the same.

"I'm Dave Howk. Your lawyer hired me. I've news of your wife. Follow me," he said and drove on.

He led him through traffic as dusk fell on the deserted industrial district in Northwest Portland. In an empty lot with broken streetlights, he slowed to a stop next to a lonely panel van he'd stolen that morning. He got out, leaned against the rear of his car and waited for Warbler to join him.

When he pulled up, Howk asked, "Did you call anyone on the way here?"

Warbler stepped out of his car, saying, "No, why? Should I bring Jerry in on this?" Jerry was the lawyer Howk had been dealing with.

Howk moved within reach. "Don't bother." he said and swung. His gloved fist made contact with his temple. He enjoyed watching him hit the ground. He followed with another blow that put him out. After he got him in the van he headed out to redneckville.

* * *

The Oregonian's lead headline read: Local Business Leader Missing. The story that followed gave the last-seen details and told of the inconclusive investigation into the missing wife. It was the future Mrs. Warbler who reported him missing when he didn't show up to take her to dinner at El Goocho. He was an hour late when she called 911, but they didn't take her seriously until the next morning.

Howk waited for the police to visit him, but after a couple of months had passed he stopped thinking about it. It wasn't until six months later that he got a call from Warbler's former lawyer, Jerry. "Guess who showed up in town, Howk? Charity Warbler.

Can you believe it? I guess I was wrong about you. No hard feelings, I hope."

"Are you her lawyer now?"

There was quiet pause. "She asked me to, but I took a pass. I know when I've been outmaneuvered."

Howk ran into her at his local lunch spot, but it wasn't a chance meeting. Charity didn't eat at lunch counter dives like this one.

"I wanted to thank you," she said, sliding into the booth across the table from him.

Howk looked at her for a long moment. She looked good, tan and rested, and he got a flash of her face from their time at the motel together. He closed his eyes and it went away. When he opened them, he said, "Your husband didn't know anything because he hadn't done anything."

"It's just like the papers said, 'Distressed wife of philandering husband disappears to pull her life together.' It's not an uncommon scenario."

"And now his money is all yours."

"Once they declare him dead, if they ever find him, but until then it's as good as, thanks to you."

He pushed what was left of his lunch away, his appetite gone. Silence filled the space between them.

Her eyes reached out for his. "I missed you."

He left her in the booth at the diner and drove to the mausoleum to visit his wife, stopping along the way at an empty field to see what wild-flowers he could find.

People Like You

I was making my way through the park when I saw a young kid, maybe in his second summer, and male from the scent of him, though the load in his diapers was doing a good job of masking that. He was sitting alone on a grassy hill in a remote part of the park, either lost after wandering off, or unwanted and dumped. I'd seen a lot in this park. It was big and wild and brought out the best and the worst in people like you. I kept an eye on him from a distance as I rolled on my back and soaked up the warmth and scents of a spring day. After watching me for a while he started down the hill in my direction. When he fell for the third time, I saved him the trouble and trotted up to him.

"What do they call you?" I asked as he reached out to scratch my fur along my back. Tall ones always want to do this. I don't know why. We don't do it to each other, but I don't mind as long as they do it nicely.

The kid made a gurgling sound in response to my question. He was probably too young to answer and too young to figure out that he shouldn't be understanding what I was saying either. I sat with him for a while, debating what to do. I had places to go, things to do, but leaving him to sit alone in his poop-filled diaper was just plain cruel. I don't know what it is about your sort that likes to keep your feces close at hand, but personally, I like to leave mine behind, preferably in the middle of a large paved area, like a driveway. What did I know, maybe he had his diapers just the way he liked them. I was saved making a decision when I heard a woman not far away calling out.

"Oh my God, where is he? Dillon?" Her voice was shrill with anxiety. I hear a lot of anxiety in my encounters with you tall ones and wonder if it has something to do with the hard surface world you've built for yourselves. A moment later she emerged from the bushes, followed by a man pulling up and buckling his jeans.

I barked to get her attention so she'd see her kid. She did and ran straight at me screaming like she was crazy. Which she was, humping away in the bushes to have another baby when she couldn't even keep track of the one she had. She probably thought I was going to eat her boy, but the smell of all that poop put me off that idea long before I got near him.

"See you later, kid," I said, then skedaddled before she got too close. Over my shoulder I saw her swoop the kid up into her arms, the movement tearing loose the diaper's tape, presenting her with prompt payment for her negligence.

* * *

She's let out of her so-called house twice a day, once in the morning and once in the evening. She drags a woman behind her by a leash for a while, then the woman drags her by the same leash back home, a ritual of conflict. The woman talks on her cell phone and ignores the dog. The dog sniffs pine cones and ignores the woman. I don't know about you but when pine cones are more interesting than me, it's time I re-evaluate what I'm doing with my life.

Every day I'm here to observe their tug-of-war ballet, not because the irony of their situation amuses me, but because the bitch is the perfect female form; muscular haunches, rumpled fur just long enough to cover her four sets of tits, still swollen from an earlier pairing. What a bitch, but unfortunately, not in heat. She's what you call a mutt since she doesn't look like any of the usual groupings you have for us, like poodle or boxer. There's something about mutts that does it for me. Maybe because they're so different than my kind. We would pass for Labradors, but we aren't, far from it. There's something exotic about the coloring of this one's fur and I want to jump her bones bad, but mixing with the indigenous stock is forbidden, an indulgence not worth the risk of being vulnerable while in a tie with some cheap piece of local talent. But there's more to it than that. It's taboo. Many find just the thought of it repulsive, equal to one of your sort jumping the fence of the zoo during off hours and giving it to one of your ancestral apes.

I'm not one of those. Taboo gets me going. I'd equate it to boinking someone really stupid, and we know that goes on all the time among your sort, but the comparison breaks down because it requires one of the pairing to be smart to start with. It doesn't take a parasite specialist to see that human brilliance wouldn't illuminate a nesting den. You have an affinity for surrounding yourself with hard surfaces that I just don't get. If you need a hard surface go find a big rock to bask on, but to actually build machines to produce liquid rock and then to spread it everywhere you live to the point where you need to build other machines to produce rubber soles for your feet so that you can venture forth from your homes out into this world of rock you've made for yourselves seems idiotic, if not just plain nuts. But what do I know, I'm just a dog from another planet.

We came many generations ago, twelve mating pairs in one of many ships scattered across the galaxy. Some believe they were given to us by the creator, others say we were put on them by a visiting alien species to get us off a planet that would soon be engulfed by its sun. It's the same debate all species have, tying their primitive past to their current understanding of the world around them. We've moved beyond urinating on trees like the indigenous canines you keep as pets to inhabiting entire worlds. We just hadn't counted on Earth already being populated with a dominant species that controlled all of its resources, nor it being a species of primate that had taken such a disturbing evolutionary turn toward destructiveness. Sure, I'll chew up a stick here and there, it's relaxing, but I don't blow up buildings, let alone cities. That's the opposite of relaxing and any species that shoots guns to relax has issues, and boy do you love your guns.

Take grass for example. What is this incessant need to cut it short? When you trim it low to the ground the way you tall ones like it you end up eating roots and dirt. You cover it with fertilizer and moss killer and can't even walk on it unless you have your rubber soles on your feet, the kind that go above your ankles. So what use is it then? You might as well have fired up your liquid rock machine and turned it loose in your yard.

The conflict ballet has reached its midpoint and the woman has begun dragging her dog back to the house. Over her cell phone, she complains about the dog. It's only now that she's become aware of the dog she'd tied herself to. I've daydreamed of playing the hero and rescuing my fluffy princess mutt from her life of twenty-minute walks and confinement by setting her free from the woman's leash, but I doubt it would end happily. She'd soon be lost and scavenging on the street and some good Samaritan would "rescue" her again and she'd end up at a shelter. There she wouldn't even get the twenty-minute walks and she'd be at the mercy of the arrival of another tall one who was willing to tether themselves to her. Humans won't always be the dominant species, at least that's what I console myself with when

I see people like you up to your tricks. One day another species will evolve and push you out like the weeds in your lawns. With a little help from me and my sort, it may even be your own dogs.

A Coke and a Smile

Dave parked his car in the far corner of the liquor store parking lot and remained behind the steering wheel with the wipers on intermittent. He went there sometimes to think. It helped put his life in perspective, where he'd been, where he was, where he might go. As he sat in the warm car watching the wipers push the rain around his windshield, he saw his girlfriend's car turn into the lot and park out front in the slot underneath the neon Budweiser sign. This couldn't be, he thought as a hand forced its way into his chest and wrapped its cold fingers around his heart. She'd been distant around him recently and this was partially why he'd come here to think. Angie got out of her car, looking good in tight black jeans, and rushed through the downpour into the liquor store. Now he knew why she'd been distant and what had come between them.

If a little was good, more had to be even better. This wasn't always true, but Dave didn't know that. Or rather he did, but didn't. A part of him denied what was true and imposed a lie and he lived by the lie telling himself it was the truth. One drink was good. Two, better. Eighteen … The mind of an addict. When

Dave quit drinking he wasn't surprised to find he had no friends who didn't drink. People who didn't drink made him uncomfortable. They weren't living the lie, or at least not his lie. His friends were and they could nod at the lie and smile that it was the truth. They respected the lie. Dave dried out on his own without the help of rehab or AA meetings. It was a shit experience and the fear of repeating it so far had been much stronger than any wish to go back to living the lie. All he had were friends who hoped he would fail so that he'd return to being their drinking buddy and stop making them uncomfortable. Only a recently quit drinker was worse to be around than a non-drinker.

Dave came from a long line of drunks and drinkers. His mom was a drunk despite that drinking killed her parents. His dad was a drinker. The difference was that the lie is even greater with a drinker. They never get smashed. They never pass out. They don't black out. But they compare themselves to people who do and say, "See? I don't have a problem." All the while it affects every aspect of their lives and they need that drink just as badly as the drunk. His dad's father didn't drink at all, but his father's father had been a bad one and probably drank enough for both of their lifetimes. Dave's sister was a drinker and her husband was a drunk and their two boys were approaching the age where they would start sneaking cans of beer from their dad's stash in the garage.

When Dave quit he tried to maintain his relationships with his mom and his sister and her husband, who were all the family he had left, but after a while the upside to that was outweighed by the downside. Drunks don't respect themselves, nor do drinkers, especially drinkers who are married to drunks; they're full of frustration, feeling that if it weren't for the drunkenness of their spouse their life wouldn't be so full of disappointments. If you don't respect yourself, you don't respect others. Dave tried stopping by his sister's house when he figured they wouldn't be drinking, but that became impossible to predict, and on the off-chance they weren't drinking they were hungover and there was their irritability to contend with. It disturbed him to see it passed down to his nephews. They were learning the coping skills, as he had from his parents, that were supposed to get them through life. The cynic in him laughed, seeing proof that the world was truly fucked, while the drunk in him cried.

Angie came out of the liquor store carrying a brown paper bag the size used for a liter bottle. Dave knew what was in it, Grey Goose, her vodka of choice back when she was a drinker. She had quit before they met, otherwise they never would've gone on a first date, and nothing had suggested any different in the six months they'd been together. He thought about what it would be like for them to drink together. It would be a lot of fun, a total blast for a week or two. He missed the freedom, the lack of inhibitions, the drunken spontaneity. But then the self-disgust would flood back with the hangovers and they'd turn their self-loathing on each other, filling each other's void with anger. He could be a drunk again and she could blame everything sour in her life on him, conveniently forgetting that she had chosen this course for them and he had been too weak to say no.

But that was not how it would be. Dave believed that if he didn't resolve his addictions in this lifetime, he would take them with him when he died, only to get saddled dealing with them again in the next life. He had lived the alcohol nightmare too many years and it had been too difficult a struggle to get to where he could cope with the world without self-medicating to toss it in and have to start from scratch in the next life. He'd beaten an addiction that had torn up his family, generation after generation. No one was worth risking that for. He'd break it off with her when he got home.

Just before she got into her car, Angie looked up, as if she felt his gaze on her, and recognized his car parked across the lot. She trotted through the rain, carrying her bottle like a baby cradled in her arms, and got into the passenger seat with a flurry of wind and raindrops.

"Doing some thinking, huh?" she said. She knew about his trips to the liquor store parking lot.

He looked at her, the cold fingers tightening around his heart, then stared at the bag in her lap.

"It's not what you think. I almost did, but I didn't." The rain pattered on the roof of the car. "I was going to buy a bottle of Grey Goose, but I couldn't. Something inside me said, 'No, don't do it.'" She pulled back the top of the brown paper bag and Dave saw the familiar red plastic cap of a liter of Coke. "I don't even like Coke, but with the way the guy behind the counter was staring at me like I was some sort of freak, I had to buy something just to appear normal." She lifted the Coke in its bag. "This was the nearest thing."

Light-headed with relief, Dave smiled. "Pass it over. I'll drink it."

Angie looked at him with raised eyebrows, knowing he disliked it as much as she did.

"At this moment," he said, "I love Coke."

How to Make a Sandwich

That's it, put some mayonnaise on it. No, don't put it away, don't be cheap, put it on with a spoon. Stop worrying about your arteries. Stress will kill you long before the mayo. What? The jar's almost empty? Well then, use it up. Oh yeah, there you go. No, don't put it in the sink, you idiot. Put it on the floor and I'll get it ready for the recycle bin. I know lettuce is good for you but let's not over-do it. Okay, I need roughage. You could play eighteen rounds with that last poop. Spray 'em white and sell 'em on eBay. Ooo pickles, I like pickles. I wonder if you could pickle a cat. Mmm, that sounds good. Let's pickle Buttons and put him on a bun. Might have to get some more mayo though. Tomato slices work, put a few more slices on. Whoops, you dropped one. Here, I'll get it for you. Slurp. Gosh, I don't see it. Where'd it go? That damn cat must've kiped it. He's fast for a fat bastard. He might even be enough for two sandwiches.

It needs more ham, more turkey. You might as well be a vegan for what you got on there now. You need protein, boy, lots of it. Okay, now it's looking good, but it could use some strawberry jam and some whipped cream and some lox. Look at all that stuff you got in the fridge you could put on it. If it won't fit on the sandwich just use the plate. Plate too small? Get a bigger plate or a serving platter.

What? That's it?! One little sandwich on one little plate? Are you insane? You'll starve and die and where will that leave me? I'll end up in the pound because of your tiny sandwich. Okay, let's go into the living room and sit down. Sure, I'll sit next to you on the couch. What's wrong? Aren't you going to share? What about living your life as an example to others? I doubt Mother Teresa would do this to her dog. Goddamit! Give me half. I was the one who showed you how to make it. You're such a pig.

Oh, the phone, that's right, go answer it you greedy bastard. Slurp, gobble, slurp, lick, lick.

Sandwich? It was the cat. I warned you he's fast. Don't look at me. No, I'm not smacking my lips. No, that's not mayonnaise on my nose. Lick. See, it was never there. In fact the sandwich was never there. You must be hungry. Come on into the kitchen with me. I'll show you how to make a sandwich. I know, I get that feeling too sometimes. D⊠jà vu, like we've done all this before.

Faking It

"Come on, sugar tits, how much for a blowjob?" the john asked.

She squeezed her knees together below her tight mini-skirt. "I already told you. I don't do that anymore. I quit."

"You don't quit being a whore, baby. Once a whore always a whore."

She'd been sitting alone at a table in Starbucks studying for her beautician's exam over a coffee when this asshole sat down across from her. It happened sometimes, the johns from before when she worked Sandy Blvd. would recognize her during daylight hours, but the norm was that after a flash of shame and guilt on their faces they'd look away and pretend she was just another stranger like everyone else, which she was, aside from that she'd had their cocks in her mouth.

"You should leave," she said.

"Shit, I've got half an hour left on my lunch break. I'm not passing this up. We could use the bathroom here. How sexy is that, getting blown in a Starbucks' john. It's been a while so I'll be quick," he added, taking his wallet out of his back pocket. He checked his cash. "How's forty bucks sound?"

Forty bucks sounded good, money always sounded good to her, but not good enough. She liked the separation between church and state, and right now she was nothing more than a normal young woman who would soon have her beautician's certificate and a job at a high-end salon in the Pearl District. She had the looks for it and the people skills. The last part she thought with a subtle smile.

"Leave now or I'll tell the management you're bothering me."

"What? You want me to tell everyone you're a whore?" His voice had risen and a middle-aged woman sitting nearby glanced over.

"You want everyone to know you get your dick sucked on Sandy Blvd.?"

He was quiet for a moment, then put his wallet away. "Fucking slut. You bitches are all the same." He got up and left, glaring at her over his shoulder as he did.

The woman nearby raised her eyebrows at her. The young woman met her gaze, then rolled her eyes, saying, "He has Mommy issues."

The woman smiled back. "Don't they all."

* * *

She hadn't been lying when she said she'd quit. It seemed ages since she'd been on Sandy Blvd. She'd worked it long enough to know it would chew her up and spit her out. If one of the johns hadn't gotten her a pimp would've. Girls didn't work Sandy without a pimp and when you had a pimp all your money went to him and he'd put you on an allowance, just enough to get by. So when she started to draw their attention she moved on to the airport hotel bars and worked them for a while.

Now she didn't need to do any of that. She had a group of regulars who called and between them and their referrals she did quite well. She provided the "girlfriend experience" and was good at it; all the benefits without the headaches. She'd listen to their shit, comfort them and screw them. The hardest part was making sure the johns didn't get too serious and fall in love with her. When that happened they wanted to be her savior, here to take her away from "all this." That wasn't love, just bad for business. She wasn't a victim and she didn't need nor want saving. That was just another variation on the pimp scenario. The victim was the john. He was the one paying an inordinate amount of money for a lie, and at times they needed to be reminded of this.

So when a john started showing signs of thinking he was in love with her, she'd introduce an evening of bondage games into his girlfriend experience. It was hard for him to think of her as someone who needed saving when he was tied spread-eagle on the bed with his balls resting in her palm. She'd tell him to say foolish things and if he refused she'd squeeze until he did.

"No, I won't say that," the john said and struggled in his restraints, so she squeezed, gently at first.

Almost a whisper, "Say it."

He grunted as she squeezed harder.

"Men's nuts are a design flaw. They make you so vulnerable." She started to twist as she squeezed. "Say it."

"Okay, okay, I'll say it." He swallowed. "I love you."

She relented and smiled. "And I you."

Initially she worried doing this might mean losing clients, but instead they called more often and she started charging them more for a "girlfriend 'plus' experience," and there was no more talk of getting her "away from all this." Love and pain had been paired and she controlled both. It did a number on her head when it came to her own relationships. None of her friends at beauty school knew what she did and it was hard for her to see the guys who asked her out as anything more than potential johns just wanting to get off. But then she met Samson.

Samson had been a referral from one of her regulars, but he hadn't come to her to have a girlfriend experience, but for sex lessons. He wanted to be good, the best, because he wanted to be a gigolo and provide the "boyfriend experience." She agreed to take him on as a student and to teach him how to please a woman. It didn't hurt that he was good looking, well endowed and took direction well. He was soft spoken with a calm personality that made being with him easy. A silent moment was simply that, not an awkward gap that needed to be filled with annoying chatter. After a few weeks of teaching him she realized she was having sex with a man without having to lie for the first time since she started providing the girlfriend experience and maybe even before that. No fake orgasms, no phony praise, no dirty talk that would leave her silent for hours afterward. She always scheduled the johns who needed the dirty talk to get off last because after them she was done, no more. It was after them that she considered quitting. But she didn't, and she kept working on Samson's technique.

She'd been telling him about orgasms and how it was important to climax together, that it created the impression of equality that was key to the afterglow, and it was while they were practicing Samson's fake orgasms that she knew she'd fallen in love with a john. Sure, she thought of him as a student learning to be what she was, but really he was still a john paying her for sex.

"You're a natural at it. You must've faked it before." They rarely shared information about their lives, but as he'd gotten better a shift had taken place that opened the doors between them.

"Sometimes it's easier. I dated this girl a while back and toward the end she just didn't do it for me. She was insecure about her breasts, well, she was insecure about a lot of things but it was her breasts she focused on. We'd be going at it, I'd be tit fucking her or something like that, and she'd suddenly say something like, "Wouldn't it be better if they were bigger?" Her boobs were fine, but once she'd say something like that I'd have to start reassuring her about how they were perfect just as they were, and that got old, fast. One minute I'm fucking her, the next I'm her fucking therapist. I wanted to fuck, not talk, so I started faking it and taking care of my business later when I was alone. We didn't last much past that. I think she was angling for me to buy her a boob job."

"Did you?"

"You kidding? I can't stand fake tits. Don't even watch porn with them."

"A lot of your middle-aged Janes perceive a little sag and off to the plastic doc for implants they go. It's something you'll have to deal with."

"Doesn't matter. I'll be faking it anyway."

"What if you get a case of the saline blues and can't keep it hard?"

He smirked at the improbability of that, then smiled and pinched her nipple. "Then I'll think of you."

"And I you."

Good Source of Food

I only had to show my last owner my teeth once in a while to stop her fat ass from crushing me on the couch, and when I say fat I mean black lab fat, golden retriever flotation device fat. I never had to bite the bitch; my growling would get her to rethink where she was going to land that thing. She must've been half blind and didn't see me, or I was small enough to blend in with all the pillows and doilies covering the couch. I did have to nip her occasionally, and I have to admit I was severely tempted to play tug with some of those folds of flab. I never worried about starving around her though, she was a good source of food.

She was some bitch, too. She had so many pups she must've popped them out for decades. Me, they cut me open and did something so I couldn't have puppies, which is totally unfair. Her litters would come over all the time, dragging their own pups with them, and she would feed them like they were never weaned. What just one of them ate in a single sitting could feed an entire litter of mine, if I'd had one. Her litter was loud and obnoxious, but they had an upside. They were food slobs. Especially the young ones.

There was this one pup they called Boobers. He was just out of diapers but they should've left him in them because I don't think he had the whole idea of pooping someplace other than where you eat figured out. Once that pup got his hands on some food he was determined to hold on to it. There was this one time when his group had come over and I was staying clear of them lying on the couch in the TV room when he came in carrying this big ol' bologna sub sandwich. Eating bologna is like eating five different animals at the same time. I love figuring out what critters are in it because they change from brand to brand. Whoever came up with it must've been a dog. So I showed Boobers my teeth and growled at him but he made no move to share his feast; he just kept taking these giant bites out of it and kind of mooing as he ate like a Jersey cow. He'd be big enough to be one with the way he was putting on the pounds. Maybe he had that gigantism gene. He must've weighed twice what other kids his age did. The way that sub was disappearing made me nervous so I went for his pant leg. I grabbed it in my teeth and started pulling and shaking it like I was a pitbull that had eaten some kid's Ritalin. Boy, I could barely budge that fat leg of his. He started crying and wailing for his mommy, but damn if he didn't keep eating between sobs. He even wiped his tears with the butt of the sub, which was now about half gone, and as I saw it, the fat bastard was now eating my half.

There was only one thing left to do. I let go of his pant leg. Showed him my teeth in one last warning to give up the sandwich, and when he went for another bite, so did I. I aimed for the soft part of his calf, which was most of it, and chomped down. He let go of that sub so fast it fell to the floor and bounced three times before I caught it and dragged it under the couch, where I could eat it in peace.

There was some fallout from Boobers' parents. His mom started saying the usual crap about needing to do something about that dog, but my owner came back with what she always said. "Well, if Boobers ate at the table instead of running around the house leaving mayonnaise all over my walls, this wouldn't happen."

It was true. Sometimes I'd have to wait over an hour for a slop of mayo from one of Boobers' sandwiches to run down the wall before my tongue could reach it, all the time hoping my owner wouldn't spot it and cheat me of my treat. I think sometimes she left it there for me to wait it out. She was nice that way. Do you know how slowly mayo moves on a cold day? It practically trickles in comparison on a summer afternoon. Whoever invented mayonnaise must've been a dog, too.

I had lived in a couple of homes before this one, starting with an old man in an apartment consisting of three consecutively smaller rooms with a shoebox for a kitchen. I don't know how anyone could live with a small kitchen. It should be the biggest room of all. Food is life. Then the bathroom was off the kitchen and that bathroom stank because the old man couldn't hit the inside of the toilet bowl with his piss at night. He tried to train me to pee and poop in a plastic tray full of kitty litter like a cat because he never wanted to go outside, just sit in his food-stained recliner in front of the television. All this was going on way too close to where I ate so I took to relieving myself underneath his bed instead.

He finally started paying a neighbor to take me out on walks and one day the neighbor took me out on a very long walk and a drive in her car and left me with another old person. This one at least liked to take me out for walks and I was halfway through training her who the furniture belonged to when she packed me up and brought me to my owner with the wide behind. It's funny how people come in all different shapes and sizes. They're as varied as us dogs.

One lazy afternoon I was eating another one of Boobers' sandwiches underneath the couch when I overheard his dad saying that the first thing he was going to do when the old lady died was take that damn dog to the pound. Well I knew who that damn dog was and I'd seen the pound on TV and it was never good. That day came sooner rather than later. The old lady went to bed and never woke up and the next thing I knew I was sharing the backseat of the car with Boobers and his dad was driving and his mom was in the copilot seat.

Her eyes were puffy from crying as she looked out the window with a lost expression on her face. Suddenly, she said, "Where are we going? This isn't the way home." I could tell her where we were going, the prison for dogs. Sandwich theft was a capital offence.

The dad was having difficulty restraining a smile. "The pound. We're dropping that dog off."

The mom shifted in her seat to face him. "Like hell we are. That dog, as you coldly call her, was my mom's best friend. She doted on her and she's my last connection to my mom. We aren't taking her anywhere but home with us. Besides, at Boobers' age it's time he had a dog."

Hearing that, I looked up at Boobers next to me and showed him my teeth. He was eating a bag of chips and had yet to share, but then without me having to growl at him he reached into the bag and offered me a very large chip. Sour cream and onion, one of my favorites. It was then that I realized that Boobers and I shared the same taste in food. Maybe he was a dog reincarnated because he mostly ate food thought up by dogs. I smiled at him again and he gave me another chip. Seeing that it was kind of small, he quickly gave me another and then ate one himself. He was exhibiting very promising behavior, sharing without having to be prompted. I'd have him trained in no time and he'd be a good source of food; his dad on the other hand would have to be put down.

The Walk-In

Wayne felt slightly off when he woke up. He felt even more off when he saw that he wasn't in his own bed. He couldn't remember the last time that had happened. This bed had red sheets with tiny black hearts. A poster of a boy band was taped to the wall, four teenage boys posing petulantly for the camera wearing black rags and sporting black die jobs, among other cutouts from fan magazines. They all looked like androgynous twerps to Wayne. He never understood the feminization of today's male. Sinatra had been more his style.

As he became more awake the significance of waking in a teenage girl's bedroom fully struck him. With a hot flash of adrenaline he glanced at the rest of the bed and was relieved to find himself alone in it. He couldn't recall a thing from last night, which meant he must've blacked out, but he didn't have a headache or feel hungover. In fact he felt really good. "Peppy" described it best and he hadn't felt peppy in over a decade. He rubbed his face with his hands, wondering how he could've got there, and suddenly froze. His face felt wrong; it was smaller, and he had no morning stubble. He had long brown hair and both his ears were pierced in multiple places. With a sinking feeling he slipped his hand inside the panties he was wearing. Oh my God, his dick, it was gone. And so were his balls. Panicked, he sat up, pushing the bed covers aside, and pushed down his underwear. His eyes bulged in disbelief. Oh my, he had a vagina. He pulled off his T-shirt. And tits, nice tits. He jumped out of bed and stood in front of the dressing mirror. He didn't just wake up in a teenage girl's bedroom, he woke up as that teenage girl, and she was hot. She would've given him wood if he still had a dick, instead he got a different tingling feeling which was pleasant in its own way. Shit, he thought, I'm getting turned on by myself. This was certainly going to make life easy.

There was a quick knock on the door and an attractive woman poked her head in, saying, "Time to get up."

Wayne looked at her face, then at his own in the mirror. They looked a lot alike. "Mom?" he said meekly.

The woman cocked her head to the side. "Honey, what are you doing?" she asked, looking at him standing naked in front of the mirror with his black panties bunched below his butt.

"Is this a dream?" he asked.

"Honey, if I woke up with your body, I'd sure say it was a dream. But you three kids changed that. I'm definitely going to the gym today."

"So this is a dream?"

"Yes, honey, this is a dream where you pull up your panties and get ready for school."

He suddenly felt self-conscious and did as she suggested. The panties felt different than the boxers he'd worn for seventy years, but not restricting because there was nothing left to restrict. Ugh, he thought.

His new mom smiled. "Well, got to wake your brothers," she said and disappeared behind the closed bedroom door. There was a robe hanging from the back of it. He slipped it on and sat on the edge of the bed to collect himself. He was a teenage girl with a milf for a mom and he had to get ready for school. Well, he could manage that. It was only a dream, after all.

He found the bathroom down the hall. From the sounds emanating from inside, it was occupied. He knocked.

"Yeah, yeah, don't get your panties in a twist," a boy's voice answered, probably one of the brothers.

He had never realized how irritating that comment was until now. "Hurry up, you little shit, I need to shower." He hadn't had to wait to shower in years. He'd really taken a slide down the economic ladder.

The door opened. "No shit, you stink," the boy said as he slipped past her.

"Asshole," he said under his breath.

Her brother glanced over his shoulder as he went down the hall. "I heard that and I'm telling Mom."

"Tell her what, you stupid fuck?"

"That you called me an asshole and a stupid fuck."

He'd gotten himself into a tit for tat with a preteen boy. What was he thinking. Normally he would've just scared the crap out of him. "She won't listen to a little brat like you."

The boy laughed. "Who do you think she's going to believe? Her good little son, her perfect child, or you, the teenage delinquent Lilo wannabe who's been grounded half her life? Duh."

He glared at the boy. "You better watch your back, fuckhead."

Their mom called from downstairs. "I heard that."

He went in to the bathroom and locked the door behind him and sat on the toilet. It sounded like the girl was a real screw-up with no respect for her elders. He hated that but it had become the norm as he'd gotten older. This was the strangest dream he'd ever had and it was the strangest thing to experience pooping as another person. She needed to eat more bran. While showering he saw a razor hanging from the bottle rack and realized he probably had to shave his legs and underarms now. He ran a hand over his legs and looked at his armpit. Boy, this girl was kind of a slag. Well, he'd help her out during his timeshare, he thought as he picked up the razor and soap. It was nice to be able to lean over without his back cramping.

After he showered and made it back to her bedroom, choosing what to wear became a problem. Her clothes said she was a slut, or at the least, a tease. Her skirts barely came below her butt and she had nothing but punk rock T-shirts. He found a pair of black jeans and a white button-down that looked practically new. The jeans were tight going on but at lest they covered his skin. The shirt was boring but at least it didn't say to the world, "I'm a slut and the line starts here." He found a pair of penny loafers and slipped them on. They were well worn, complete with pennies. What did he care if his clothes were exciting or not. He had never even thought of clothes in those terms. They simply covered his nakedness, kept him warm, or at worst made you stick out, like wearing a U of O Ducks shirt to a Beavers game. He'd done that unintentionally once and ended up having to turn the shirt inside out to get out of there without getting into a fight. The Beavers were losing.

He looked himself over in the dressing mirror and realized he did care if his clothes were exciting or not, as if the girl's interest in clothes had bled into his personality. She hated the shoes. They belonged to a uniform, and then it dawned on him that he wore a uniform to school. He opened the closet again and there it was, shirt, skirt and jacket and socks all hanging from the same clothes hanger. There was a school crest on the jacket. Oh no, he thought, it was the nuns all over again. She went to St. Mary's Academy. There was a backpack on a small writing desk cluttered with makeup bottles. He picked it up and emptied it onto the bed. She was a senior, her name was Olivia, and from the looks of her doodles, extremely depressed. He picked up a spiral notebook that was filled with her writing and was hit with a flood of her memories filtering through his own. She hated the uniform; it reminded her of hairy nuns and creepy pale-skinned priests. Her classes were boring, the girls were stupid, and her mom was a bitch who wanted her to be a younger version of her boring self so she could marry some jerk like her dad and her mom was pissed because she was prettier and hotter than her even with all her goth makeup.

Wayne was two people, an aging retiree annoyed with a body failing him a bit more each day and frustrated with the need for naps like a small child, and a sprightly girl with her whole life ahead of her but depressed enough to think that life was just a bunch of crap. Just for a moment, he couldn't remember his name, not Olivia, but Wayne, and it was as if he, Wayne, was the passenger. Her body and returning memories confirmed this. His memories of being Wayne were fading; his dead wife, his grown kids were all disappearing behind a cloudbank of Olivia's monotonous days at school, fights with her mom about her clothes, and one last memory of a bottle of pills held desperately in her hand.

He found the empty bottle between the bed and the wall. It had held a hundred sleeping pills. He hid it in her backpack, ashamed for her, and as he looked at himself in the mirror, he saw Olivia, and Olivia saw herself and Wayne was no longer there. She scratched her head with both hands and shook it to clear it. God, what a strange dream, waking up as a strange old man in her body. She wondered what the nuns would make of it. Boy, he sure did miss his dick. She felt her crotch and could almost remember what it was like to have one. She knew what the nuns would make of that.

She quickly dressed in her uniform and as she put her books back in her pack she found the empty pill bottle. She dropped it back into the pack, figuring she'd throw it away at school. Then she opened up the spiral notebook and turned to the last page. It was a note to her family. She tore it out and tore it up, then wadded it into a ball and dropped it into her pack. She'd throw it away at school, too. She didn't know what she'd been thinking. She had less than a year left of the nuns, and if she got a job she could move out of her parents' house. But if she was nice, maybe they would send her to college. She'd been thinking so short term and wasteful. Now she had her whole life ahead of her and she was going to live it right. The old man would want her to.

Swallow It

It was raining on that first Christmas since moving back to Portland, that distinct Portland drizzle that is less than rain but more than mist, much like in the Scottish Highlands but without the romance. I ate Christmas dinner at my brother-in-law's parents' house. It was an extended gathering of his and my sister's family. It was one of those scenes where you know everyone, but only enough for it to be uncomfortable when the banter falters. I don't follow the big three sports, especially not the U of O Ducks, but if I had the evening would've been a breeze. This was the fallback topic when you had no interest in the other person, easy conversation when you were halfway through a box of Gallo's finest. It was a booze fest. Everyone but the kids had a glow on. So on a day that was pitched as being meaningful, nothing meaningful would be said. I couldn't tell you how many times my mother had drunkenly told me she loved me only to be totally uptight the next day as if nothing had been said. It started early when I was a kid, and I absorbed that lesson well. What people say when they're drunk doesn't mean shit.

Both my parents like to drink and it was from them that I learned to drink and learned that it was how we coped with the troubles life sent our way. If someone hurt you, you reached for the bottle and swallowed it. You did not face the trouble and deal with it because if you did that the whole family would come apart. If my parents stopped drinking, they'd get divorced, and that was what eventually happened. My dad quit for a while, but my mom kept on and that was the end of their marriage. My mom always kept on. She'd get stumbling drunk and never acknowledge it, as if that would make it like it never happened. But it did, again and again, and it left its mark. I hated sloppy drunks. So I drank, but never got sloppy. After a certain amount I would go home and drink alone, really swallow my pain, and there no one would see me stumble to the fridge for another beer or pass out in my armchair with the DVD player repeating the same setup program again and again.

It was while living in Boston that I got into the full swing of it. The depressions would set in like the fog on Boston Harbor, my eyelids would feel heavy and my thoughts sluggish, and the only way to burn the depressions off was to get drunk and lose myself. I'd find an Irish pub in the North End and start in on the Guinness and Camel filters until I dulled the edge on my dark mood. After that I'd hit a few other bars where my friends hung out and be out until it didn't matter if I was out or not. I was running from my mood, but, like Buckaroo Bonsai said, "No matter where you go, there you are."

I gave up the booze and cigarettes because that was a candle I'd burned from both ends, wax was all around my feet and the two flames were about to meet. Now it was a bunch of little things I was hooked on, none of them as destructive as the booze, but it all felt like I'd slid from one addiction to another as easily as slipping on comfortable shoes after work, and all to avoid being home. Not home in the sense of sitting in my living room, but home inside my head dealing with my thoughts and fears and anxieties.

Here I was in my forties trying to fill the same unmet emotional needs I began experiencing when I was a boy. Thirty-odd years of beating my head against the same problem had burned me out. I'd come up with answers here and there but they did more to reshape the problem than to solve it. The core of it was self-worth. I'd do stupid stuff to undermine myself and to confirm that I wasn't worth other people's love, but it was more complicated than that. I didn't respect most of the people I knew. I didn't disrespect them, I just felt that respect was earned by acts of emotional courage and strength and I saw very little of that in the people around me. Much in my life had been about emulation, so my flawed thinking went that if others didn't deserve respect, then I didn't either, nor should I do anything that earned that respect. Few faced their demons. Most avoided them as I had back when I used to drink, and though I could empathize with why they did, I didn't feel sympathy for them. Instead I avoided them just as they avoided their demons.

When I faced my alcoholism for what it was, a dead-end escape route of slow suicide, and quit the booze, hanging out with my friends was old. They would metamorphose into boring drunks, and without being tight myself, listening to their self-inflicted trials and tribulations was too much like listening to the hamster complain about being on the wheel. When I got past the self-abuse of the drinking and cigarettes I thought that would be it. All I'd have to do was not drink or smoke and my life would heal and all would be okay, but addiction peels away like an onion and my body had to clear itself of the physical effects before I faced what got me hooked in the first place. I thought the addiction was to the booze, but the booze was only a tool.

I didn't have to be a drunk to be an addict. Drunks were messy and thus easy to spot. When I quit, my understanding of addiction matured and I saw it as driven by a fear of being alone with myself, and that it came in many guises, shopping on eBay, pints of chocolate Häagen Dazs, cycling to exhaustion, just to name a few, and I saw addicts everywhere. When I quit smoking my sense of smell returned and I noticed smells I hadn't in years. When I quit drinking it was as if another sense had returned too. I began seeing the addiction in the people around me without trying. One friend ate sugary foods she knew would leave her depleted and in pain the next day but ate them anyway because she felt she deserved to feel that pain. She was unworthy of feeling otherwise and her body took these feelings and thoughts and manifested them by attacking itself. I had an overweight friend on a similar cycle, and a riding buddy who dulled his pain with shopping for high-end bike components.

It was the same for myself, and it was why my addiction had found new ways to undermine my self-respect through pointless crap that I didn't care about as long as it was a momentary escape from the depressions and confirmation that I didn't deserve even my own respect. Self-respect was the basis of happiness, but I couldn't be happy. I didn't respect myself because I'd never learned to love myself; in fact, I'd been taught just the opposite. The drunken words of my mother would run through my head and if it was something she could only say when she was drunk then it probably wasn't true. I knew my current crop of addictions were more dead-end escapes like the booze had been, more layers of the onion, but now I was realizing that the morning I quit drinking was actually when I began to learn to love myself. I stopped swallowing the pain and began facing it. I figured I'd eventually work through it and be done with it, and then maybe I could shape my life into something more like I'd imagined it to be as a kid.

* * *

At Christmas dinner I sat at the dining table next to my mother and ate my turkey and watched the wine go down all around the table. I watched my two young nephews ask if they could taste my sister's wine. She said sure, go ahead, and I could see their future arced out in front of them. They were learning the same coping skills I had learned and were learning them well. I left as soon as it was polite to leave and when I got out into the cold air and into my car, I felt a rush of anger and pain and wanted to turn it in on myself like I used to when I drank. I wanted to go down to Fred Meyer's, pick up a suitcase of beer and drink it down, swallow my pain.

Slug Boy

The rain tapped against the bathroom window as Abby showered before getting ready for work. She was soaping her legs when she noticed a dark mark, like a swipe from a brown magic marker, on the tile wall. That's weird, she thought, how could that get there? She leaned in through the steam to get a closer look.

"Oh crap," she said to herself with a start. "There's a baby slug in my shower."

At first she was grossed out, and for some reason having the slug in her shower while she was naked made her feel vulnerable, as if somehow it could get her because she was without her clothes. As if clothes could protect me from a slug, she thought, and then stopped herself.

"What am I thinking? God, I'm afraid of a slug."

It was tiny, the size of a matchstick. She assumed it was a baby because she was only used to seeing the big ones on sidewalks but for all she knew it could be full-grown. She hadn't thought much about slugs and didn't know they came in all sorts of sizes. In fact, she knew very little about slugs. It had tiny antennae that searched the air in front of it as it climbed the tiles to get clear of the spray from the showerhead. Now that she was no longer startled, she wouldn't say they were cute, but the way they moved was intriguing. Where did the slug come from? Maybe the recent days of downpours had driven it inside, or maybe it had come up from the shower drain? Ugh, she thought, I'm being invaded by slugs through my drain.

She started to worry the shower spray would wash it clear of the wall and it would swirl down the drain to drown. She didn't wish drowning on anything, even a gooey slug in her shower that had caught her naked. She had a fear of drowning, that and house fires, and just thinking of them gave her chills. Maybe she'd been accused of being a witch in a past life and had failed the water and burn test. But what was she going to do with it? She didn't want to touch it, and even if she did, she wasn't going to give the fat man who lived behind her a show by running outside naked to find it a new home. So she did nothing. She directed the showerhead to minimize the spray in the slug's direction, then finished her shower and stepped out of the stall to towel off. She left the shower curtain pulled to the side, thinking the stall would dry out and the slug would go in search of a damper climate. But she didn't know what it liked or what it would do so she put it out of her mind and got ready for work.

* * *

The next morning when she showered before work she didn't see the slug and figured leaving the curtain open for the stall to dry out had worked, but the following few mornings it was back and then one morning it was much higher up the wall, about eye level with her. There was no way she could shower without the spray hitting it so she decided to move it, but when she touched it with her fingertip to flick it into her palm, it was much more strongly attached to the wall than she had expected and she decided to leave it alone and went about her bathing. When she glanced at it again, it was gone. She checked by her feet, but it was nowhere to be seen.

"Oh," she said sadly, realizing she'd grown accustomed to the slug. "It's gone down the drain. Shoot."

She tried not to picture it drowning, but it really bothered her and she couldn't. Wanting to be free of the water and her thoughts, she quickly finished her shower and got out, but throughout the day, the slug kept popping into her mind. In the middle of making a series of client callbacks on the phone, she started wondering where slugs went when they died. Was there a slug heaven for slugs that had been good? What about a slug hell? Could slugs even be good or bad? She was lost in her moral dilemma over slugs and it carried her thoughts to her own mortality, wondering where she would go when she died. Would it be the same place as slugs? Did Jesus have a position on slugs in Heaven?

She'd read that people lived forever and only their bodies died and then they got a new one and were here at work again. She liked that idea until she considered where she'd be when she was between bodies. Would she get a loaner until her new one was ready? No one took care of loaners cars and they smelled of other people's bad habits. Or would she float around bodiless without her boobs and pretty smile? She felt her smile was her best feature, which was why she smiled a lot, that and she had noticed it was contagious and she would much rather deal with a smiling person than a grinch. Maybe her next body would have a nice smile, too.

Her work desk was in a maze of cubicles, and as she was thinking this, Nathan, a coworker she found exceedingly annoying, started down her aisle interrupting everyone to show them a printout of his wife's ultrasound. Then it struck her how precarious this theory about getting a new body could be. With a squeamishness that went all the way down to her toes she realized if she died today she could come back as Nathan's kid.

When Nathan arrived at her cubicle, announcing what he had to show her, she forced a smile as she took the offered picture and asked, "When's it due?"

"It?"

"Yeah."

"It is not an it. It is a he."

"Oh, sorry."

"He's due on the sixth of January."

"Boy, you know the exact date."

"It's called science, Abby."

She handed back the picture.

"But we might induce labor early so we can claim him on this year's tax return. I'm going to love having a dependent."

He moved on to the next aisle over, and she said aloud to herself, "I can do that."

"What can you do?" It was Anne, with whom she shared her cubicle, returning with their coffees.

"Stay alive until January seventh so I don't get reborn as Nathan's kid."

"Oh, God, can you imagine?"

"That's my problem, I can."

"Ooo, ga-ga," Anne cooed like a baby. "I wuv you, Daddy."

"Stop, please."

* * *

The next morning in the shower her slug was back. "Hi, Mr. Slug," she said. All slugs were male to her. "I thought you were dead."

And then, as if purposefully, the slug let go of the wall, fell to the floor and swirled down the drain before she could even react.

"Shit," she said. "Goodbye again, Mr. Slug."

If he'd been a good slug, maybe he'd move up a few notches and come back as Nathan's kid. Or he might crawl up out of the drain and be back tomorrow, trying to be as good a slug as he can so when he dies he won't come back as Nathan's kid, she thought with a smile, her best feature.

Rain Check

"You can't put the shaving cream back in the can," James said. Lola was sitting across from him in Java PDX. Sunday morning jazz tinkled in the background. His feelings for her had been growing for the past year and he craved to be with her, but they were only friends.

"What am I going to do?" Lola said, her eyes tense, searching his for an answer, one hand kneading the palm of the other.

"It's not like what you said isn't true." Her mother *was* self-absorbed. In the year or so that Lola had been sharing stories about her mother with him, her mother had rarely showed interest in others, especially her daughters, unless it served her interest in some way. Her mother would invite her to a family dinner, then say hardly a word to her. It just wouldn't look right if one of her children didn't show up, somehow make her appear less a mother. And then the following weeks after Lola's show of support at dinner, she wouldn't hear from her until she wanted something from her again.

James was glad she'd finally stood up to her mother. "You're just the first to get so fed up with her that you spoke your mind.

You know your sisters are thinking it too but are too scared of her to say anything."

"Yeah, but I'd been drinking and it was ugly." She looked down at her hands, still kneading one with the other. She wanted a way out. She didn't want to stir this pot with her mother and kicked herself for doing so. "What an ugly thing to say to my own mother. No one wants a mother like that."

What she'd said to her mother James had heard her say before many times and worse. It was obvious that was how Lola felt about her. She needed to accept that, and maybe her mother had needed to hear it. "Don't take this the wrong way, but maybe you're less ashamed about saying it than you are shocked at how true it sounded when you said it. Sometimes when we say it aloud to the person it makes it real."

She looked up from her hands. "It's pretty damned real this morning. When I woke up and remembered what I'd said, I broke out in a sweat."

"Now you've said it, it's out there and can't be taken back, but you're trying to. If you can make yourself into the bad one here, maybe it'll mean what you said wasn't true, or better yet, you can blame yourself, that you've somehow made her into the cold, hard woman she is." James felt a release inside himself as he said what he had to say. His dislike for Lola's mother had been building, but more so had his frustration with Lola for not being able to see her mother for the bitch she was and shake off the rude stuff she pulled on her. He couldn't understand why she let her walk on her that way.

"Well, I've got news for you," he continued, letting his passion get the better of him. "That's bull crap. You're just working it to find some way to blame yourself because if you can blame yourself then it's not her fault and you can keep on hoping that she'll change. Well, I've got more news for you. That's more bull crap. She's sixty-some years old and she is who she is. You've got nothing to do with it. You're not responsible for your mother or for why she acts the way she does. It just hurts because you're realizing that she's nowhere near the mother you'd hoped for. You probably had friends as a kid who had mothers who were nice and kind and warm and did things for their kids and you wondered why your mom didn't treat you that way. Any self-help book will tell you that was where you learned to blame yourself, that something must be wrong with you. That's why your mom was a bitch, and ever since you've been blaming yourself and trying to make it up to her, but now that's getting hard to believe. You got drunk and told her the truth that had been bubbling to the surface through all the lies you've been telling yourself over the years. And again it hurts because you've begun to see through all those lies you've based your sense of yourself on since you were a kid."

He didn't notice the change in her expression or he would've stopped. He was too wrapped up in feeling right and saying what had to be said. "You know, all this pain and blame could've been averted if your mother had been able to show you a little love when you were a kid. But she didn't. That doesn't mean there's something wrong with you. The truth of it is that it hasn't been your mom holding you back all these years. She's nothing more than an enabler. You've held yourself back by undermining yourself. That's good news, though, because that just leaves yourself to change. You may not be able to change your mom, but you can change how she affects you." He'd said more than he'd wanted, but it needed saying and it might as well be said now.

Lola was taken aback. It was if he'd popped a balloon and her guts had splattered all over the table between them. "Sounds like a speech you've been practicing," she said coldly. Nobody liked being dissected so openly.

A nervous laugh escaped his lips. He had practiced it, silently in his head every time she reenacted one of the encounters with her mother. The old woman bullied Lola with her criticisms into being the insecure daughter she needed to prop up her ailing image as the loving matriarch. She was as much a loving matriarch as he was. He'd never been so direct in telling Lola what he thought of her and her mother, figuring it was something best left alone, but his frustration with her slow progress in breaking free had made him think she needed a push. He wouldn't admit it to himself, but he felt her mother was what stood between him and Lola getting together. As long as she was under her mother's thumb, she wouldn't be whole enough to be with him. Instead he painted it with righteous, broad stokes. There were too many lies holding people back and he'd reached his limit.

The cold look on Lola's face that was reminiscent of her mother said he'd said too much. He now felt as she did, wishing he could turn back time and pluck his words from the air before they reached her ears.

Lola seemed to be waiting for a response. He didn't really have one. "I guess I have been practicing it, in a way. I just wish you could be free of her and see yourself for who you really are."

"But you just said it was me who …" but she shook her head not wanting to argue it with him. In a matter of seconds he'd revealed himself as not her friend, but as another player trying manipulate her in his direction.

"I'm sorry if I've gotten into your business too much," he said, and even as he said it it sounded lame.

She looked at him, feeling the way she did when she looked at her mother. She was at a crossroads. The role she played with her mother no longer fit, and what James had said rang true in her ears, but it pained her that he saw her as such an emotional weakling. He was going at her like her mother did, just from a different direction. She was filled with anger at her mother and at herself for trusting her mother and it would've been very easy to switch her dependence from her to James. He at least seemed to want to guide her out of the pain to become a fuller person, but a fuller person in whose eyes?

And then from the deep recesses of her mind she heard a voice say, "He could be your daddy." That stopped her. She'd heard that tiny voice before and had ignored it, only to realize later that it had been right. She wasn't going to trade a bitch of a mother for a father figure with his own agenda that she'd be expected to live up to and get stuck playing the role of the pupil, always trying to please someone else. She'd been that too long. She was tired of waiting to hear someone else's opinion just to make it her own.

She stopped kneading her palm and pushed away her coffee. She was tired of lacking the confidence in her own abilities to manage her life. But it was more than that. She was disgusted with herself for being more comfortable as her mother's lackey than confident enough to be herself. She was so comfortable in that role that she could sense she was quite willing to con herself into thinking that becoming James's lackey would be a step forward, when in fact it would be trading one monster for another. He'd be nice in the beginning but eventually she wouldn't be what he wanted and he'd start in with the carrots and the sticks trying to change her into someone she wasn't. He played it like he was Mr. Nice and accepted her for who she was, but she'd learned from her mother. In the end it was about control, like trading one cult leader for another, and even though she felt herself to be a natural born-follower, it was time she was her own monster.

"Well, thanks for listening to me," she said, emotionally withdrawing from him. It was time to go. "I know I can be a bit of a broken record when it comes to my mom."

He felt it, too, her pulling away. He'd said too much too soon. But it would always be too much too soon. She was saving him from being what he most despised, people like her mother, people like his own mother. James and Lola weren't meant to be, and they both felt the truth of it hanging in the air between them like a brief snow flurry melting on the wet asphalt.

"Are we still on for tonight?" he asked, knowing they weren't.

"Another time, maybe. How about a rain check."

Good Morning

Daisy and Posie always checked in with each other the mornings after bar hopping.

Saturday morning:

"I told him to piss off and die. What else could I have said? He was stealing my underwear, dirty ones at that. What a freak."

"I would've gone for the clean ones."

"Well, you're considerate in that way. I tell you, I have the worst taste in guys. What is wrong with me?"

"Posie, it's not like your vetting process is very strenuous. You met him at the Virginia Café at around ten-thirty and by one you're doing the nasty with him. Why'd you take him to your place, anyway?"

"What do you think?"

"Still living in his old room at his parents' house, eh?"

"You got it."

"On the bright side, he was cute. Was he any good? He must've been if you let him stay over."

"Ha! I wanted him to leave afterward, but he had no way to get home, so I told him I'd give him a ride home in the morning.

That was until I woke to him sniffing my underwear and stuffing them into his jeans pocket. What a thing to wake up to. Freak."

"Were they those new pink ones you bought at Victoria's Secret last time we were there?"

"Yeah."

"At least he has taste. Those are cute."

"On me, yeah, but not on him. Eew."

* * *

Sunday morning:

"I was stuck. I couldn't move at all. There wasn't an ounce of fat on him but he weighed a ton."

"Muscle weighs more than fat."

"So I've heard. There he was, hard as a rock inside me and he passes out in mid thrust. At first I'm like, dude, what's up? Why are you stopping? And then he starts to snore. God, I've never been so insulted. I know these idiots pass out to porn, but the real stuff? What's the world coming to? He wouldn't wake up. All I could do was squirm."

"Squirm?"

"Well, you know, why waste it? And it was there, ready to go, and it's not like he objected. Besides, I hadn't brought him home for his conversation."

"Your place again?"

"Yeah."

"Don't tell me, still living in his old room at home?"

"Nope. That got converted to a study. When he moved back in it was into the basement with the washer and dryer. In the car on the way to my place he kept going on about how he couldn't believe his parents would do that to his room. I shut him up fast once we got inside and then he goes and passes out on me. What a loser."

"Ah, don't be so hard on him. He had a long, tough week. Maybe his mom likes to do his laundry at night, you know, send junior a message. How'd you finally get him off you?"

"The pencil pinch between his fingers like my dad used to do to wake the drunks when he was walking the beat. Christ, listen to me. I'm sleeping with guys my dad would think were drunks."

"Cute drunks with pretty muscles."

"There's nothing cute about snoring."

"Did he wax his chest? He looked the sort to wax his chest."

"Would you stop? I'm serious, Daisy. We need to find some guys who aren't losers."

"Let's try that place on Fifth where all the stockbrokers go."

* * *

Thursday morning:

"I don't know, I kind of liked it. He wasn't in such a hurry to stick it in. He took his time getting there, know what I mean?"

"But he did get there? Mr. Limpy didn't show up from a bout of conscience over cheating on his wife and two-point-five kids?"

"He wasn't wearing a ring."

"Was there a tan line on his ring finger?"

"Tan line? Where do you think we are, California?"

"What was his place like? Was it a mess?"

"I didn't see it."

"No, you didn't? You took him to your place."

"He said his place was being redone."

"Yeah, redone with diapers and pacifiers. Did he stay over?"

"He cuddled for a bit then said he had an early start. Did you know the markets open at six here? He has to be at the office at five. I could never get up in time for work that early."

"Someone trained him to cuddle. Any idea who?"

"He asked to use the shower before leaving."

"His wife has been doing the training. That makes you the other woman. How's it feel to be a home wrecker?"

"It's not my fault his wife's sewn her twat shut."

"That's awful."

"Well if she were taking care of her man he wouldn't be out there making fools of girls like me. Asshole."

"True, but you can't really expect too much from someone who can be led around the room by a pair of tits. I thought he was going to follow you into the bathroom."

"What about you and his friend's ass. You wouldn't shut up about it."

"His ass made me want to put a mirror on my ceiling."

There was a pause, then they said in unison, "Target?"

"Sure, after work."

* * *

Saturday morning:

"He had a pimple on his left cheek. All those hundreds of squats or whatever he does for the perfect ass and it's ruined by a pimple. I just couldn't get past it. I was ready to tear that mirror right off the ceiling."

"So much for liftoff."

"Wait, you don't think I give up that easy? What do you think make-up is for?"

"You didn't?"

"I did, and off I went. That mirror was the best forty bucks I've spent in a long time. Told him to hit Tanarama a few times and to give me a call."

"Will he?"

"Without a doubt. I asked him about your guy and yes, he's married with kids. He has two and one on the way. He made it a point to tell me how awful he thought his friend was for cheating, but he was just giving me lip service. I put him to work to shut him up. What about you?"

"When he asked to shower before leaving, I told him it was broken."

"I bet he didn't like that."

"No. I won't be hearing from him again. I'm giving the stockbroker place a wide berth for a while."

"That's fine with me. The older guy routine isn't really for me anyway."

"Back to our macho wannabes?"

"Do you want a puppy you can train from scratch, or a dog loaded down with baggage from the previous owner's screw ups?"

"Well, if you put it that way."

"But did I mention housetraining?"

The Chicken or the Egg

The Spigot was a cinderblock bar that from the outside looked more like a pump house than a place of business. It had a single story with no windows, a front way in, a back way out, and was surrounded by a parking lot and dead shrubs. Once inside there was no way of knowing whether it was day or night, sunny or cold outside. After a while there were some at the bar who didn't even know if the outside still existed.

"We all poison ourselves in one way or another," said Dean, a fat man pulling a cigarette from his pack on the bar. "I just choose physical forms that everyone, well everyone not in denial, acknowledges are poisons. Cigarettes, whiskey, beer, though some may argue that beer has nutritional value that exempts it from being a poison. Although beer is no fun unless you drink poisonous amounts of it."

The man on his left raised his bottle of Miller an inch off the bar. "Hear, hear to that," he said.

"There are plenty of emotional poisons far worse than anything Jack here could serve up," the fat man said, jerking his chin at the bartender listening in on the conversation.

The man on his right wagged his head over his glass of scotch. "Uh oh, here comes another one about the ex-wife."

"You're exactly right, my friend. After about a year of marriage Daria started nagging me about all my vices, which I never understood because it's not like they were new vices. I drank and smoked and loved to eat long before I met her, so she knew what she was getting when she married me. But when I learned about her father and mother it all fell into place."

"You've never mentioned them before," the man on his right said, lifting his scotch to his lips.

"I've got your attention now. See, it's not all drivel about the ex. Her dad liked to eat and drink and smoke, much like me, but heart disease got him and he died in his fifties. Now Daria will tell you her dad died of this—" the fat man punctuated his words with his still unlit cigarette, "—and booze and greasy bar food. No offense, Jack."

"None taken," the bartender said.

"But it was his wife who killed him. Daria's mother nagged him about his so-called bad habits until her words were poison in his ear, and he made the mistake of letting her get to him. She was unhappy. She wasn't married to Clark Gable, so she went about trying to change him, and he was less changeable than me, and since he wouldn't bend to her will, she poisoned him with her stress and constant disapproval."

The man on his left coughed into a bar napkin. "They say laughter can cure cancer."

The fat man lit up. "You're damn right it can, and it's the pointless stress in your life that gives it to you." He exhaled smoke into the smoky room. "So there I was playing my part in a depressing tableau from the dreary past of my wife's family."

"Ex-wife."

Dean lifted his whiskey glass an inch off the bar. "Hear, hear to that," he said and raised the glass to his lips and sipped. "And my role in this drama of hers was to die from the stress she was laying on me so she could prove her bitch of a mother a saint. As if repeating the same mistake in the next generation made it right, instead of twice as fucked up. Well, I put a cork in that bottle of emotional poison and divorced her ass. She took me for half of everything, even joint custody on the dog, but that was a price worth paying to stay alive."

The men at his sides raised their drinks an inch off the bar. "Hear, hear."

"Jack, let me buy a round for these great Americans."

"Back at you," the men at his sides said and finished their drinks.

When the new round was served, each man lifted his drink and said, "Here's to great Americans."

They drank, then the fat man said, "Now that I've done the ex-wife, next topic."

"How about those commies in City Hall?"

The fat man licked the whiskey off his lips. "Are you sure you want to get me started on those bastards?"

* * *

The Grape was a wine bar downtown on Broadway catering to the after-five crowd. It didn't have happy hours, but did have local wines on sale depending on what vineyard the managers were pushing. Daria and her friend were sharing a bottle of Riesling that was sweeter than what they usually went for but they'd wanted to try something new. They were seated in a booth at the window in the sun where they could crack jokes at the bad suit and tie combos passing by.

"There's one for you," Daria said. "Wide and yellow, straight out of the seveties."

"He'd try to sell you a used car on your first date," her friend said.

"When I was in college," Daria said, "the relationship books that were all the rage said you'd marry your father or you'd marry your mother and I always said I wasn't going to do that. I wasn't going to marry my father, and then years later, there I was, married to a man just like my father."

"I remember those books," her friend said. "Marriage One-oh-one. That one bounced around the sorority for a while."

"My dad was an overweight alcoholic who didn't take care of himself and left it to my mother to do it for him, like a child who wouldn't grow up. Dean was exactly the same. I'd fix something healthy for dinner, like lemon chicken and broccoli, and he'd grumble about when was I going to start cooking some real food, like mac & cheese and burgers. Christ, he loved that stuff. The image of him gorging himself is seared on my mind."

"You could feed a family of four on the calories alone."

"When he realized I wasn't going to fix that poison anymore he started eating at the pub before coming home, and that got to be later and later. Why get married if your husband is down at the pub all the time? Christ, he was married to the bottle long before he married me. That's what I don't get. How could I fall for a guy who was so wrong for me?"

"Those fad books explain that."

"I never read past the part of marrying your dad. I read that bit and thought, crap, I don't need to read this. I'm not so stupid as to marry a fat drunk. My husband was going to be cute and slim and smart. But the books were right, for me at least. But there was more to it than just marrying my dad, I also started behaving like my mother. I used to hate how she nagged my dad all the time. Sure, he had a lot of problems, but he wasn't a mean drunk or anything like that. He was the stereotype of the fat and happy man, but my mom was a mean nag; she still is. My dad lost his ready smile and kind of wilted under her relentless pecking. He was like a shriveled party balloon weighed down by its string."

"That's so sad."

"I'd smell the booze on Dean when he'd come through the door and I'd start in on him. I'd become my mother and I couldn't help it. It was like if someone pulls at your arm your impulse is to pull back. Dean would act like a loser and I would just start pecking at him. He just wouldn't look after himself and it was like I was reliving my childhood through my mother's eyes. Christ, it was depressing. I cried so much about it. I couldn't believe the happiness I felt on our wedding day had led to that, that my marriage was nothing more than acting out the crappy roles we'd learned from our parents."

"Tell me about it."

"When Dean asked for a divorce, I was hurt and angry. He never tried to make it work. He always got his way. But later I realized that if I'd stayed with him I would've hardened into being a bitter lady like my mom, disappointed in my failed life. She's such an uncompromising nag, always critical. I used to figure it was my dad who made her that way because he was such a child, but maybe he acted like a child to rebel against her being such a …"

"Hard ass?"

"That's one way to put it. I called her the other day, excited to tell her about something at work, and crap, I'll never do that again. I went from happy about life to depressed in a five-minute conversation. Christ, she pushes my buttons."

"The chicken or the egg. Which came first?"

"That's exactly it. Would they have been any different with someone else or was it a ballet they were destined to dance? Well in my case, Dean's definitely the egg because if he was the chicken he'd eat the egg and we wouldn't be having this conversation."

"So who's this new guy you've met?"

"Oh, he's nothing like Dean or my father. He's cute and slim and …"

"Smart?" her friend suggested.

"Yeah," Daria said and they shared a laugh. "I can't believe I just said that. Can you imagine marrying your dad twice?"

"Duh? Daria, what do you think I did?"

Unfriended

The cancer did what cancer does, it whittled Skid's father down until he was ready for death and then one morning Skid's sister went into the room where they'd been caring for him in her house and his body was there but whatever made her dad her dad was gone. His eyes were open and staring out the window as if still seeing the birds he used to watch. His expression wasn't sad or happy or in pain, just empty. He was gone. She tried to close his eyes like she'd seen done so many times in the movies and on television but nothing was like in the movies and especially not like on television and they wouldn't stay closed. When Skid arrived, he was still looking out the window, but with half-closed eyes.

Their father had been the emotional glue that bound everyone together. Skid had been close to his father his entire life, and with his father gone the ties to his sisters and mother came undone. There wasn't enough there on their own to hold them together. Besides being family and sharing history, they had little in common. In fact it was what they had in common that pushed them apart. Skid got hooked on booze in high school and drank his way to forty when the self-medication with the drink stopped cutting it and it was either upgrade to a more potent drug or quit and deal with the pain that had led him to embrace booze in the first place. It seemed overwhelming and doomed to fail like the times he'd tried to quit before, but he chose the pain.

His family was full of drunks. His dad had been an alcoholic, the functioning kind. His mom was a drunk, the slur your words and then deny she'd ever been drunk kind. Both her parents had been drunks who died in a fire because they were drunk. His younger sister was the functioning kind but too selfish to quit herself when her husband, the get really drunk kind, tried to quit. His family was much like her own and Skid saw it as the two great houses of drunks joining together to create the ultimate drunks, but their boys were too young to show the promise their breeding gave them. His older sister was an alcoholic too, but she was the manic kind who would binge, then not get out of bed for days on end. She'd married a social drinker she'd met during a period of sobriety and he looked after her. In a sense enabling her to binge. Someone had to bring her food in bed when she wouldn't get out of it except to pee.

The only blood relative in his family who hadn't been an alcoholic had been his paternal grandfather whose father had been such a bad drunk it had put him off drink from the beginning. When Skid quit drinking he was quiet about it. He wasn't going to preach about it when chances were he'd be back at it soon enough. But when he started turning down drinks they soon figured out he'd quit, and when they would ask him and he'd answer yes, their awkward body language said they'd been hoping for a different answer, like maybe he had a cold. It was okay to quit for a cold. That was fine. They'd quickly move away and it was not a problem to find someone who hadn't quit, because no one else had. Talking to him put them in troublesome territory. It made them think about their own drinking and most everyone who drinks to self-medicate knows they have a problem with it but spends much of their energy denying it to themselves and surrounding themselves with like-minded problem drinkers who'll back them up when they say things like

"No, I don't have a problem."

Or,

"I can quit any time I want."

And Skid's two favorites,

"Yes, I'm happy."

"No, I never get depressed."

When Skid's dad was diagnosed with cancer it pulled everyone together, but his death exposed the falsehood and relations quickly returned to their previous state of slow demise. Skid didn't want to be around them when they drank, but they wanted him at family gatherings like Thanksgiving and Christmas. The first Thanksgiving after his dad died he went to his brother-in-law's parents' house where they were all gathering. He made it through dinner but didn't stay long afterward. Being around all that self-destructive behavior was such a downer that he chose not to go to Christmas dinner or any other family gathering. He caught a lot of flack for it and they were angry at him for not coming. It was about appearances. They wanted him there because it put him in collusion with their lie that nothing was wrong and there wasn't a problem. His presence allowed them not to acknowledge the guilt they chased away with every drink. But his presence also made them uncomfortable because he'd quietly acknowledged that there was a problem and inwardly he became paired with the problem to the point that he became the problem. Nobody wants to talk to a sober person when they're not. It makes them too self-conscious and reminds them that they could be much more than what they are. He was a threat. He'd faced the fears they ran from.

Skid sensed their awkwardness and their avoidance. They'd made a point of getting him there, had said hello, and then ignored or avoided him. When he stopped going to family functions he had a hunch they were as much relieved as he was. When he explained to his mother that he wasn't coming to Christmas because he found being around the alcoholic behavior depressing her reaction woke him up.

"I'm disappointed," she'd said.

"You're disappointed? In what? In me?" He was shocked at the selfishness that she exuded. "You're disappointed in me because I'm choosing not to drink and don't want to be around a bunch of people who drink to excess every chance they get?"

"I just wish you could just get over it."

"No you don't. You wish I'd go back to drinking and pretend like nothing was wrong."

No one had his interest in mind, especially not his mother, because his absence from family gatherings made her look worst of all. Her selfishness made him angry. He was trying to take care of himself and all he wanted was her support, but the anger was the same he'd felt as a kid and had been running from ever since he took that first drink. In a roomful of drunks telling each other lies, he was the one she thought should change. He used to talk about this stuff with his dad who had quit drinking a few months before his diagnosis. Now with no one to talk with about it who shared his views, Skid felt like an outcast, the nail in the board everyone was trying to hammer down. He could've gone back to drinking then and this period of sobriety would be forgotten and never mentioned again, like a bad dream everyone wanted to forget. They'd embrace him into the fold and make sure his cup was always full. But he didn't go back to drinking. He chose not to be around them at all, not even when they weren't drinking. He wasn't cutting them out, as in not speaking to them, he just wasn't going out of his way to hang out with them. When he explained it to his younger sister, her level of anger shouldn't have surprised him, but it did. She unfriended him on Facebook, and when he noticed this, he started laughing and it was the laughter of relief. If you're going to be that way about it, Skid thought, then good riddance.

Skid was a drunk. He drank his way out to the edge and lived there for years with his feet dangling over the side, but then he quit and crawled back and confronted the emotional wounds that he'd run from in the first place. Now, having been sober for several years, he didn't want to be around people who hadn't done or weren't trying to do the same. People could tell themselves whatever lies they wanted and find plenty of fools to believe them, but he could see through it because he'd been there, but wasn't any longer. So when his father died it was a release for Skid, too. He wasn't tied to the past. He could call a lie a lie and let go. And that was what he did.

13978629R00129

Printed in Great Britain
by Amazon.co.uk, Ltd.,
Marston Gate.